Christmas Eve™

and the

Golden Garland

of Zeus

by George Broderick, Jr.

for lovers of whimsey
and adventure everywhere.

Chapter One

"I don't mind telling you, I'm a little scared," stammered Noel.

This was a most unusual statement for the little Sugar Plum Fairy to make. Noel had always been the brave one. She was what her fellow sugar plums liked to call "uncompromisingly feisty". Generally, it was Carol who was the most timid of the trio, though Holly had been known to get fearful from time to time, usually about things that were spiraling out of her control. Holly was all about maintaining control and a sense of order. But not Noel. Brave, fearless Noel, looking deceptively ladylike in her fairy dress of soft browns and deep, warm reds, with her kinky ebon-dark hair done up in two, big puff balls on either side of her impish head, was just as likely to be wrestling with a polar bear cub as flitting about adding glisten to snow crystals or sprinkling holiday scents of cinnamon and freshly baked cookies in the breeze or any of the other standard fairy pastimes.

"There's nothing to be scared of," remarked Holly in that officious way that let everyone know that she was the leader of the trio.

Holly, looking cool and unflappable in her many shades of green, gave off an air of professionalism in everything she did. Her dark green tunic and skirt were always crisply pressed. Her verdant nails were always clean and her pale mint green skin was always freshly scrubbed, especially behind her pointed little elfish ears. Even her Kelly green ponytail bobbed back and forth in an almost authoritarian way, if such a thing were possible. For Holly, the most difficult fairy duties to perform were unnecessary giggling and being Sugar Plum silly.

"Maybe there'll be fudge! I love fudge!" chirped Carol in her usual, seemingly oblivious, fashion.

Carol was the best loved of the three of them. How could anyone not love Carol? From her pale pink skin to her rich, cascading magenta hair to her dark lavender fairy dress, she fairly radiated cuteness. Carol loved life and passed that love along in the way that only a true innocent could. When you were around Carol, you just felt glad to be alive. But like many bright, bubbly things, Carol was a bit unfocused. Her fairy magic was wild and undisciplined, a constant source of annoyance to Holly and an often times gateway to mischief for Noel.

But this morning was different. This morning the girls were expected to be on their best behavior, not an easy task for three silly little fairies.

As the huge oaken doors, resplendent with gold trim filigree, opened to reveal a long hallway with dark, velvety red deep pile carpeting running wall-to-wall the length of the corridor, dimly lit by glowing embers in ornate bronze sconces staggered along both walls every few feet, the girls lost all sense of decorum and began excitedly buzzing around in an agitated, somewhat distracting flight pattern. Their tiny fairy wings beat wildly, causing just enough of a breeze to make the flames in the braziers dance with an excited glee that perfectly mirrored their own. They were fairly bursting with giddiness. They couldn't help themselves. How could anyone, really? It wasn't every day that one was summoned... well, "summoned" is perhaps too harsh a word; let's say "invited"... it wasn't every day that one was invited into the offices of the big man himself, Santa Claus!

"Girls! Settle!" came the voice from within the eye of the Sugar Plum Fairies' frantic flight hurricane.

This was Christmas Eve.

Eve was a statuesque, hauntingly beautiful, poised young woman who seemed to be in her early twenties, though how could you really determine age for someone like Eve? Though not an immortal as was Santa Claus or legendarily long lived like her Sugar Plum Fairy friends or Santa's elves, Eve was nonetheless a being of pure magic and, as such, defied the natural laws that the rest of us living in Girl and Boy Land cling to so unwaveringly.

As the fairies calmed down at the sound of Eve's commanding, yet reassuring voice, Eve began the long walk down the corridor, her black, patent leather, calf high, high-heel boots barely disturbing the nap of the plush carpet. In fact, the relative quiet of her gait belied the commanding nature of her strides. The only sounds she made were a slight rustling of her short red, white trimmed silk figure skater's dress, which looked more like a Christmas tree skirt than any actual piece of fashion wear, and the crisp flapping of her Hunter green, high collared cloak, which seemed for all the world to be lined along the edges with white fur of the purest ermine but, in actuality, was trimmed with faux fur made from finely woven elfish nylon, which was steadfastly in keeping with Eve's personal convictions against harming animals just for the sake of fashion. The cloak was fastened to her collar by two clasps that resembled small Christmas tree ornaments and was joined in the middle with a ceramic chain carved to look like a popcorn string from a Victorian Christmas tree. She wore candy cane striped leggings, which perfectly matched her red tunic, trimmed at the neck and wrists in purest snow white. A bold, stylized Christmas tree emblem emblazoned her chest, completing her look as a superhero, the champion of yuletide cheer. Holly sprig earrings, which reflected the hue of her warm green eyes, added just the right splash of color amidst her flowing icicle white-blue platinum hair, which tumbled and cascaded behind her as she walked. She was followed close behind by the Sugar Plum fairies, now contritely flittering in a straight line formation.

As the three Sugar Plum Fairies tried to collect their wits and steel themselves for the upcoming meeting, they thought back on how that morning's events had led to this moment.

The day began much like any other, with Eve making pancakes for the four of them. Across the room, Noel was setting the table with their finest holiday plates and dishes, sporting cheerful snowmen and dancing gingerbread men cavorting across red and green rimmed snow fields, while Carol was carelessly pouring juice and licking spilt syrup from her chubby little fingers. Just as Holly had finished doling out equal amounts of strawberries, blueberries and powdered sugar at each place setting and was about to launch into her fifth dissertation that morning about the virtues of a nutritious breakfast being the most important meal of the day, there came a loud fervent knocking at the door of their Swiss chalet headquarters.

Eve breezed casually past the three fairies, who had all become entangled, arms and legs akimbo, sticky and smelling of maple syrup, in a raucous tussle over which of them would answer the door first. Ignoring the sisterly squabbling, Christmas Eve opened the door and there on the front porch stood Comet, one of Santa's reindeer. Fast as the celestial phenomenon he was named after, Comet was the designated messenger for all important North Pole correspondence.

"Why, Comet! What a nice surprise!" bubbled Eve "would you like to join us for some breakfast? We're having pancakes, but I'm sure we can come up with some grains for you… maybe some un-cooked oatmeal? Or marzipan… your favorite!"

Comet nickered and shook his head, indicating "no thank you" in his most polite reindeer sign language. It was then that Christmas Eve noticed the envelope held tight in the mannerly beast's mouth. Eve gently removed the envelope and, his task completed, Comet reared up in a cheery "goodbye" and took off for home. As the Sugar Plums, finally extricated from their three way scuffle, appre-ciatively, but boisterously, watched the flying reindeer swoop and barrel roll over the curving horizon, they never heard the audible gasp coming from Eve, who had just opened and read the letter.

"Now, THAT'S what I'm talkin', 'bout!" smirked Holly, "Look at him go!"

"Aw, I could fly like that if I wanted to, I betcha," groused Noel.

"I like marzipan, too, Eve! Can I have some…? Eve! What's the matter?" remarked Carol, finally noticing Eve's surprised expression as she read the letter.

"We've been asked to the castle, girls! Let's put away the breakfast dishes and head out!" breathed Eve excitedly.

The girls' reverie of frenzied preparations and a frantic flight to the big Christmas castle ended with them suddenly remembering exactly where they were and their nervousness returned them to the here and now, walking into the main hall of the magic palace and past the immense oaken doors which led down the long hallway to the CEO's office.

As Eve neared the end of the hallway, her stealthy, quiet as a gentle Christmas night snowfall stroll caught Santa's Major Domo, a dour elf called Tinselbottom, completely by surprise. He fairly leapt out of his pointed navy blue boots with surprise, performing a double mid-air somersault and landing, unceremoniously, on his gold leotard clad backside, the little silver jingle bells decorating the fringed bottom of his royal blue tunic making a most undignified, cacophonous jangling noise. With his blue and gold tasseled hat tilted across his bald head in a most disheveled fashion, Tinselbottom tried clumsily to regain his composure and make it seem as though his acrobatics had been executed on purpose. He rose slowly and gathered up his clipboard and feathered quill pen, which had flown wildly from his grasp minutes before, in a casual, deliberate manner, while simultaneously straightening his wrinkled tunic and brushing away lint and carpet fibers picked up during his startled aerial flailing.

"What are THEY doing here?" he groused, trying to shift the focus away from himself. "Santa sent for you, Christmas Eve, NOT your silly fairy friends!"

"I realize they're probably much sillier than someone in your position, Tinselbottom," remarked Eve, trying to stifle a warm chuckle. "But they have always been of great help to me in the past. I'm sure Santa won't mind."

"Very well," huffed Tinselbottom, now mostly composed except for his white beard, which bristled like a house cat that had been caught in the act of climbing the drapes and had then been squirted with water, "I shall announce you."

As the large oaken doors swung slowly open, a genuine warmth poured out from the room, accompanied by the sweet, comforting smells of Christmas. Scents of fresh pine needles, cinnamon, peppermint, warm fresh-baked cookies and just a hint of roasting chestnuts wafted into the hallway, infusing and overwhelming the senses of Eve and her fairy companions. The ambient light of the corridor gave way to the joyous blinking of icicle lights backed up by the sort of soft, flickering candlelight that makes one think of Christmas Eve services at church. The resonance of a faithfully ticking grandfather clock, gurgling and hissing bubble lights, softly rustling paper, distant chimes, crackling fireplace embers and the low click-clacking of toy trains blended together in an ear-pleasing symphony of familiar sounds . In the center of the room, surrounded by charts and maps and globes stood an ornately carved mahogany desk with a massive velvet-lined, cushioned chair. Sitting in the chair was a sprightly, stout man clad head to toe in red velvet and white fur save for his black boots and belt and hunter green gloves, his red tasseled cap tossed jauntily over one of the chair's carved bronze posts. The inundating combination of all these sights and sounds caused the return of the Fairies' earlier nervousness and all three bashfully hid behind Eve's flowing green cloak. The man looked up, over his glasses, at his guests with a mischievous twinkle in his eye and a warmhearted chuckle on his droll, beard encircled lips.

"Welcome! Welcome, Christmas Eve! Come in and have a seat! And what's this I see? You've brought three lovely young ladies with you! Splendid! Splendid! Tinselbottom, hot cocoa and warm sugar cookies for my guests!"

The four friends found themselves in the presence of Santa Claus! This wonderful, jolly man was the living embodiment of every small child's dream and the personification of every adult's wish for peace, love and happiness. In short, Santa was everything you'd ever hoped he'd be. But today, Santa was not the right jolly old elf of song and legend. Today, Santa Claus was worried.

"I'm very glad you could come here today, Christmas Eve. I have a terrible problem that I fear only you can help me with!" said Santa, gingerly skirting around an issue that he seemed reluctant to talk about.

"A terrible problem!" gasped Holly.

"Yipes Stripes!" exclaimed Noel.

"Oh my! Are you out of FUDGE, Santa? That's prob'ly the most terrible-est thing I can think of," wailed Carol.

"CAROL!" reprimanded Holly and Noel.

"Girls!" snapped Eve in an uncharacteristically harsh tone.

"Oh, ho ho!" replied Santa, "I only wish it were something as 'terrible' as running out of fudge or crumbled gingerbread cookies or candy canes without stripes. No, little Carol, this is much worse."

Santa hunched over the desk, glancing furtively from side to side, as he motioned for Eve and the girls to draw closer. He cleared his throat and began in a barely audible whisper, as if speaking his secret dread out loud would make a bad situation that much worse.

"I need your help in recovering a very old holiday relic, Christmas Eve. A relic that, if not returned, could change the face of my enterprises here at the North Pole… forever."

"Tell me, sir," whispered Eve, "what's happened that has you so frightened?"

Santa straightened up in his chair, steeling himself for what he was about to say, knowing full well that if Eve couldn't help him out of his dilemma, his effectiveness as the world's goodwill ambassador of Christmas would be destroyed from that day ever onward. After a brief pause that seemed to last an eternity, Santa spoke in a sad, baleful voice that shocked and scared him nearly as much as it did Eve and the Sugar Plum Fairies.

"Charlie the Yeti has stolen The Golden Garland of Zeus!" blurted Santa.

"Oh Dear!" cried Eve.

"Oh, my!" sobbed Holly.

"Whoa, Mama!" bawled Noel.

"About that fudge…" queried Carol?

END CHAPTER ONE

Chapter Two

Blitzen was skittish as Christmas Eve dismounted from the stalwart reindeer's back. Sure, she COULD have made the flight herself under her own power. Flying was second nature to Christmas Eve. She WAS endowed with "missile toes", after all. But following the exacting directions needed to find their present location would have taken some time and, right now, time was of the essence. Blitzen had made the trip before and knew precisely where the gateway into "The Fade" was located, so he volunteered to escort Eve and the girls to the mystic nexus, even though the entire region surrounding The Fade filled him with that unnamed dread that only animals seem able to sense.

"Are we there, Blitzen?" asked Christmas Eve, "Can you show me where the gateway to The Fade is, boy?"

Blitzen pawed the hard-packed snow, lowered his head, snorted anxiously and pointed his antlers towards a tumbledown stile just left of an ice-choked, languidly flowing rill, and slightly to the right of a copse of fir trees. It was one of those odd little splintered plank structures that escape notice until one paused to ponder what it was originally intended to surround, where the rest of it was, when it was built and why it was abandoned in such shameful disrepair. Regardless of these questions, however, Eve mused that it was nothing particularly special to look at. It was conspicuous by its very ordinariness.

"Are you sure, fellah?" quizzed Eve, "it just looks like a rickety, broken down fence to me."

Blitzen snapped his head skyward and trumpeted loud and long. He began nervously prancing around the clearing and nudging Eve with his snout towards the dilapidated boundary marker. His ears pricked up and he flicked his tail in an agitated manner. He was never surer of anything in his life and he didn't like his proximity to the gateway one bit, especially without the protective cover of the Golden Garland.

"Okay, Blitzen, I believe you. We'll take it from here. You can report back to Santa that we've made it this far," said Eve.

The words had no sooner left Eve's lips than Blitzen took off for home, pausing only long enough to lick Eve's hand and snort a re-lieved goodbye to the Sugar Plum Fairies. He wished them well on their perilous quest, but he was glad to be gone from that bleak valley. As the plucky reindeer vanished over the horizon, Christmas Eve took stock of their surroundings and formulated a plan for how she and the girls would continue.

"It's getting too dark to travel much farther today, girls," observed Eve, "let's build a fire and seek shelter for the night in that grove of evergreens."

Before very long, Christmas Eve, Holly, Noel and Carol had fash-ioned a crude lean to out of evergreen branches and had carefully built a roaring fire within a ring of medium sized rocks. Whatever provisions they needed could be gained from the inner pouch of Eve's marvelous, magical cloak which was made from the same mystic Elfin material as Santa's seemingly bottomless toy sack, the inner pouches functioning in roughly the same manner as Santa's bag, holding many times their size and weight of whatever Eve needed to make someone's Christmas bright. Eve's special cape allowed the four friends to travel quickly without the cumbersome added weight of packs, food stuffs and bed rolls. This evening, in addition to bed rolls and pillows, Eve had conjured a hearty, nutri-tious meal of zesty Irish stew, warm sourdough bread, mugs of hot cider and Dutch apple pie for dessert. After they had all eaten their fills, cleaned the dishes in the nearby stream and deposited everything back in the cape's secret pocket, they settled down for the night in their sleeping bags, around the fire and began to review the day's events.

"Santa seemed pretty upset by that ol' missing garland thingy, huh Eve?" started Holly.

"Upset? He was downright honkin' mad!" snorted Noel, "He was ready to go Holly Jolly Old School on somebody's heinie, for sure!"

Noel was right, of course. Santa was angry, an emotion which was not common for the plump sprite. His anger, too, was mixed with a fair amount of fear. It wasn't so much the theft of the garland, disastrous as that was, that had Santa so disquieted but, rather, just who had stolen it. A Yeti. If their neighbors, the Yetis, were growing as bold as to attempt such an audacious heist, what would the future of their tenuous relationship with Santa's people be like?

The North Pole folk had little use for the Yetis. Uncouth, unkempt boorish creatures, the Yetis certainly earned their nickname of the "abominable" snowmen. But, outside of a few loutish pranks involving reindeer droppings, burning paper bags and hastily rung doorbells and the occasional hurled rock, the Yetis, traditionally, pretty much kept to themselves on the windward side of the Bittercold Mountain chain that surrounded Christmas Valley. In fact, they generally ventured into Christmas Valley only in early December in an exodus of feigned penitence, trying to mooch holiday goodies from the bighearted denizens of Santa's close knit community. The Christmas folk knew it was all pretty much an act but, being the kind and generous souls they were, they, the elves especially, always saved a few scraps of gingerbread or raggedy left over dolls or little red wagons with at least one wobbly wheel throughout the year, which they gave cheerily to their malodorous neighbors. The Yetis, in turn, left the North Pole inhabitants alone for most of the rest of the year and hardly ever tried to eat the reindeer. This annual routine had become an expected part of the season and both the Christmas Village citizenry and the Yetis were content with the implied "arrangement".

Except for Charlie. Charlie was a particularly odious beast. Eight feet tall from his large scraggly bare feet, past his massive lederhosen festooned torso to the tip of his Alpine cap adorned head, Charlie was malice personified. Charlie was mean just for the sake of being mean. Even the other Yetis kept Charlie at a gangly, hairy arm's length.

Why Charlie was so contrary, no one knew. Some say it was from having to raise himself alone and embittered when his parents were killed in an avalanche. Others believed it had something to do with his poor dental hygiene and rotting incisors. Old Haggai the Yeti said it was due to a misspent childhood of pool halls, drag racing and cigarettes. But Old Haggai also believed in UFOs and something called "the infield fly rule", so most of the other Yetis took little stock in what Old Haggai had to say. Whatever the reason, however, everyone agreed that Charlie was bad news. So, it should have come as no surprise that on that moonless night, day before last, Charlie had stolen into Santa's Castle and made off with the Golden Garland of Zeus.

"Why is this Golden Garland so important, Santa?" asked Eve.

"Yeah! Couldn't you just replace it with some holly branches or mistletoe wreaths or something?" cracked Noel.

"Or a string of popcorn! I love popcorn!" offered Carol, "except when it gets stuck between my teeth. That kinda hurts."

"Well, if you'd floss properly after every meal…" huffed Holly.

"Not now, girls!" scolded Eve, "Please continue, sir."

"Thank you, Eve," continued Santa, "to properly understand the magnitude of this theft, I'll have to reveal one of my most closely guarded secrets… the answer to how I'm able to make it all the way around the world in one night!"

"Whoa, mamma!" whispered Noel.

"Whoa, mamma, indeed," chuckled Santa, "long, long ago, I found that my annual flight was covering more and more terrain and as the population grew worldwide, my reindeer team, fast as they were, just couldn't keep up with the rising demand on my resources. I needed to find a newer, streamlined way to get my presents to every good child across the planet. For the first year or two, flying opposite to the International Dateline and gaining a day helped, but that, too, soon became unworkable.

"I tried to cut a deal with Father Time, but the old stick-in-the-mud was quite pedantic about the laws of time and space and wouldn't budge. Things were starting to look mighty grim for yours truly. But just when my situation was at its darkest, one of my older elves, a forthright little fellow by the name of Sprinkles, suggested that I try to forge a route through "The Fade".

"The Fade is the name given to the realm of legend. More specifically, when a legend or folk hero's fame fades away and people stop believing or lose faith in them or they become urban legends or the stuff of conspiracy theories, they "retire" into The Fade to live out the rest of their days in relative peace and faded glory. The Fade is an extra-dimensional realm that runs parallel to the "real world" but, most importantly, exists outside the earthly confines of time. So…"

The wind howled menacingly as snow swirled all around the lean-to, threatening to douse the fire, rousing Eve and the girls from their dreamy reverie. The night in the tiny forest glen was growing more inhospitable by the moment and the Sugar Plum Fairies were becoming more frightened with every gust of bitingly chill air. Eve stirred the fire and added more wood until a pleasant, warming blaze once again engulfed their modest camp. The girls snuggled closer together, nuzzling into the folds of Eve's cloak. When they were all toasty warm, Eve spoke up softly in an effort to quell the girls' fears and help quiet the shriek of the blustery gales.

"Tomorrow, we enter The Fade, girls," murmured Eve, "Remember what Santa told us about the things we might find there…"

Eve's soft, mesmerizing voice lulled the girls back into their interrupted reminiscence. The calming image of Santa loomed large again in their brains. Carol, in particular, remembered the wonderfully tasty vanilla fudge Santa had brought into them along with steaming mugs of hot cocoa and snowman-shaped sugar cookies with green and red sprinkles. It almost made Santa's narrative seem more like a bedtime story than a tale of woe.

"So," continued Santa, "following Sprinkles' advice, I took my sleigh, reindeer and all, and journeyed to the main gateway to The Fade, hoping to make a dry run before Christmas. The reindeer grew jumpier the closer we came to the stile, hidden along the tundra between a sluggish rill and a thicket of evergreen trees, nickering, rearing and bucking about in spite of my firm hand on the reins. But, despite their trepidation, with a crack of my whip, we entered The Fade.

"To my delight, I found that Sprinkles' assertions were correct and my team was able to cover vast leagues of distance in mere seconds. With an ancient map that Sprinkles had provided to guide me through The Fade, I traveled from realm to mystic realm, darting in and out of real time. It was a heady experience and, most importantly, seemed a viable solution to my problem. Things were going swimmingly… until I came to the area that was home to fabled Mount Olympus.

"At the foot of that imposing, cloud covered mountain, my team suddenly stopped, as if lassoed with an invisible rope. They reared and struggled against their intangible bonds for some while, furiously rocking the sleigh and jostling me about violently in my seat. Then, just as suddenly as they began, the reindeer calmed down, lay down on the green-sward and nodded off to sleep. Try as I might, I could not rouse my pets from their hibernation. Then, just as my frustration was reaching its peak, dark clouds began to roll in from the mountaintop, flashing lightning and roaring with thunder. Abruptly, Zeus, ruler of the ancient Greek gods, appeared from within the flashing maelstrom! He cut an imposing figure, let me tell you! His feet were clad in sandals of the finest calves' leather and his massive form was clothed in a tunic of the most opulent spun silk, trimmed in gold and adorned with polished bronze wristbands and girded with a belt of the purest silver, etched with lightning bolt symbols, which were mirrored on his kingly scepter. His temples were wreathed in a garland of authentic hammered gold leaves and his eyes flashed cold with blazing reflections of the storm mounting within. His bold red beard bristled with anger and his voice rumbled when he spoke.

"'Who dares disturb majestic Olympus without paying tribute to Zeus the mighty?' he bellowed. I remained calm and tried to explain who I was and what my purpose was and how my trespass was unintentional, but Zeus was having none of it. With a wave of the aforementioned scepter, I and my team were engulfed in a scintilla of light, accompanied by booming thunder claps. In an instant, we found ourselves in the middle of a half-moon shaped plaza, encircled by marble Ionic columns and Parthenon-like seating. In the stands sat the cream of legendary lore. The remainder of the Olympian pantheon, fronted by Hermes, Aphrodite and Herakles, cloistered together at the foot of Zeus' grand box. Scattered throughout the gathering were Odin and his Norse coterie, led by Thor and scheming Loki, representatives of the Sasquatch nation (distant cousins to the Yetis), Manatou and Coyote from Native American lore, Paul Bunyan, a delegation of Freemen from fabled Atlantis, Gilgamesh, Elvis, the Loch Ness Monster, Robin Hood, the trickster monkey from Asian fables, Pecos Bill, Montezuma and a cadre of Aztecs from Mexico, The Jersey Devil, several unicorns, a recently thawed out Walt Disney, Lilith, Kings Kamehameha and Arthur, Polyphemus the Cyclops, Anantsi the Spider from African myth, and even the Purple Pasha of Persia. They all looked grim and foreboding. I was in trouble. Santa Claus was on trial!"

"I don't like spiders!" wailed Carol from deep within her sleeping bag, stirring the others from their remembering, "Why couldn't 'Nancy' be a puppy? I like puppies! This is the scary part of Santa's story!"

"Carol!" mewled Holly, "This is the important part! Try to focus! Santa's in real trouble!"

"I bet Santa gets twenty to life, huh, Eve!" scoffed Noel.

"You know better than that, Noel!" chided Christmas Eve, "We just talked to Santa this morning."

"Oh, yeah. I forgetted," acquiesced Noel.

"Now, hush!" reprimanded Eve, "Let's try to remember exactly what Santa told us."

As Eve attempted to curtail the girls' nervous fidgeting by speaking in reassuring, melodic whispers, the Sugar Plum Fairies did their best to remember back to that morning in the castle and the rest of Santa's narrative.

"Seems that trespassing was a pretty serious crime to the fine denizens of The Fade," quipped Santa, "and, as we say down at the reindeer stables, I'd stepped in it good this time! Zeus appeared on the dais, along with his wife, Hera and a limping dwarf, whom I later learned was Hephaestus, blacksmith to the gods and crafter of Zeus' thunderbolts, and called the proceedings to order.

"'We have in our midst, dear friends, a viper, who wantonly conspired to run roughshod throughout our many kingdoms without so much as a "by your leave'",' began Zeus haughtily. He was playing to the crowd, most of whom seemed bored to tears with the whole affair. I thought perhaps I could get a pass based solely on general apathy, but that wasn't in the cards for me. Zeus wasn't letting this one go. He continued his tirade more forcefully.

"'Many of you here see these charges as being frivolous, having secured your own reputations through flouting the law and rebelling against authority,' Zeus proclaimed with just a hint of condescension in his voice, casting a look at Sinbad The Sailor and Robin Hood and their motley crews, 'but I say to you that disdaining us in so cavalier a manner diminishes our achievements and trivializes our well-deserved legendary status!'

"That last bit did the trick! It was bad enough that most of these folk had been sent into The Fade through no fault of their own, but Zeus had just made the case that my simple mistaken encroachment was, in fact, a purposeful attempt to render them… irrelevant! The worst crime against a one-time hero you could commit! I was up against it, for sure. My only hope was that some of them might believe the truth. So, that's exactly what I told them.

"I started out by telling them all about how the one, true living God of creation, the one above them all, so loved mankind that He sent His only Son down to live amongst men as the savior of men, born of woman and God. I explained how this joyous virgin birth is celebrated throughout the world as a festival of profound love and peace. I told all who would listen about my place in the Christmas celebration and my role as the official ambassador of cheer and goodwill. I told them about unconditional giving, as exemplified by the three wise kings from the east. I told them about the happiness and laughter shared by good children everywhere. I told them all about the little child in all of us and of the child that we celebrate on that day, who makes it possible for all mankind to meet the Father. I told them everything. Yes, I told them. Now, if they would only listen."

END CHAPTER TWO

Chapter Three

As Eve took a break to stir the fire, she could see in the light from the burning embers that she was murmuring to herself, the girls having long since nodded off into comfortable slumber, Noel snoring like a chainsaw with sinusitis. Eve herself was feeling a bit drowsy, as well. She wanted to sleep. Morning would come soon and their quest would begin in earnest.

"But," she mused to herself, "there are many details of Santa's story still to go over and I want to be sure I have all my facts straight before we just blunder into things."

So, with the fire banked for the remainder of the night and the girls sound asleep, contentedly snuggling near her, Eve began again to review the morning's meeting, whispering quietly to herself and the wind.

"Holly! Stop looking at my 'Naughty List'," rebuked Santa, stopping his account long enough to refill his mug and chide the little fairy, "your 'tsk tsk'-ing at every name is messing with my concentration!"

"Sorry, Santa," apologized the embarrassed Sugar Plum, "please continue your story. I'll behave."

"Ho Ho Ho, no worries, little one," said Santa, scratching his bearded chin and sipping cocoa thoughtfully, "Now, where was I?"

"Oh, yes, I had just laid out my case for Christmas and was examining the assemblage for some sign that my story had gotten through to them. There were some indications of success. The Loch Ness Monster was softly sobbing to herself, Paul Bunyan, Elvis and Walt Disney began harmonizing 'No Place Like Home For The Holidays' and Loki was nervously fingering a whoopee cushion as if he were having second thoughts about putting it on Thor's seat, but for most of them it appeared that my defense had had no impact at all.

"Finally, after long minutes of uncomfortable silence, Zeus leaned over and whispered something in Hephaestus' ear, to which the lame dwarf responded by chuckling to himself and scampering off behind the tapestry that adorned the back of the platform. Zeus stood, very imperiously, and cleared his throat. The gathering all turned towards the imposing Greek deity. I was pretty worried, let me tell you.

"'Approach me, Saint Nicholas, you who are called Santa Claus,' Zeus rumbled, 'I have made my ruling!' I strode up to the foot of Zeus' marble pedestal, expecting the worst. Then I saw a smile cross Hera's lips.

"'Your story has touched us,' continued Zeus, 'and we are all aware of the living God, Creator of us all, and his magnificent gift. It is to this gift of love that I now pay fealty. My ruling in the matter of The Fade versus Santa Claus is thus… from this day ever after, Santa Claus shall be permitted free reign to traverse The Fade and all its varied realms, unencumbered, on his annual journey of gift giving and merriment. Further, as an everlasting sign of his safe passage and as our gift in honor of the Christ child, I present him with this token of our sincerest esteem. I have spoken! Let none who dwell herein dare defy the word of Zeus!

"With that, the Olympian motioned with his scepter and, from behind a curtain, Hephaestus appeared, carrying the Golden

Garland of Zeus. Made from the purest spun gold, the glittering swag radiated like dawn sunlight and bathed the entire amphitheatre in a warm glow of bright happiness. No one remained unaffected by the fabulous gift and all pledged their respect to this new symbol. The Golden Garland was my ticket to ride!

"As some of Hephaestus' slave workers were attaching the garland to the outer rim of my sleigh, I heard an oddly familiar voice coming from behind me.

'That worked out rather well, wouldn't you say, Santa?'

"I turned to see, to my dumbfounded amazement, Sprinkles, the very elf that first suggested I enter, and provided me with the map to, The Fade! 'What a splendid piece of mischief this was,' he clucked, 'but I knew these stiffs would come around! Their predictability is epic!'

"'Sprinkles, what..?' I started, but was quickly interrupted by the cavorting little man. 'Please, Santa! I've just engineered possibly your greatest coup! The means to travel the entire world in one night! What a joyous delight! Surely, you can call me by my right name! Rumplestiltskin, most elfin resident of The Fade, at your service, sir!'

"'But how..?' I continued, bewildered, 'Why..?

"'I've always loved children, Santa,' he said, 'and, sadly, my past attempts to get a child of my own ended badly. Ever since I came to The Fade, I've been searching for a bit of personal redemption for my prior misdeeds and, too, I admired your mission and wanted to help in some small way. Long story short, I impersonated a Christmas elf to bring about what I thought to be a splendidly workable plan. Plus, who do you think taught Hephaestus how to spin straw into gold in the first place?'

"'Just remember, he concluded, 'the denizens of The Fade are mercurial in nature and apt to change their minds on a whim. Never attempt to journey here WITHOUT Zeus' Golden Garland!'

"With that, Rumplestiltskin pranced off into the crowd, waving a cheerful goodbye as he went. He was happy to have received atonement after all this time and I now had the means to carry on my yearly undertaking. A true Christmas miracle. But Charlie the Yeti threatens all that with his heinous theft of the Garland. I need help Christmas Eve. The help that only someone of your heroic stature can provide. Will you help me?"

"It would be my honor, Santa," replied Christmas Eve.

With her own words echoing through her mind, along with flashes of their preparations and trip to the stile astride Blitzen, Christmas Eve's head grew leaden and weary. She had mulled Santa's narration over in her brain and had gleaned every shred of information she could harvest, hoping that it would be enough to help her and the girls on their quest. For now, it would have to be. The night was growing long and she would need the rest, she reasoned, if she were to be at her best. Tonight, sleep, she thought, for tomorrow they enter The Fade and their perilous trek begins in earnest. With these thoughts bobbing through her waning consciousness, Christmas Eve drifted off into a sound sleep.

Eve awoke to the sounds of giggling and the raucous splattering of a full bore snowball fight. As one of the slushy missiles whizzed past her head, Eve sat up, rubbing the sleep from her eyes, just in time to witness Noel take one in the back of the head. Holly and Carol giggled uncontrollably as Noel did a little jig, trying to dislodge the ice crystals from inside her dress, where they'd slid down her neck to take up frosty residence along her spine.

"My, but aren't we frisky for so early in the morning," trilled Eve playfully.

From the position of the sun, Eve could tell it was still early, maybe just a little past dawn. She rose and put away the bed rolls into her remarkable cape's pouch, stirred the dying embers to heat the cinders and added kindling to stoke the fire so they could all have breakfast before beginning the day's arduous journey. But a sudden splat across her back rudely alerted her to the fact that she had become embroiled in the girls' winter war. Eve stood erect and, with her fists firmly placed on her hips, let out a stern, authoritarian "ahem". The Sugar Plum Fairies stopped their tomfoolery and apologetically gathered at Eve's feet, contrite expressions on all their faces. When they were all reluctantly assembled, Eve broke into an impish grin and shook the snow from the overhanging lean-to branches onto the girls' heads in a flurry of playful retaliation. Then, amid a volley of snowy projectiles and laughter, Christmas Eve made her way to the clear, burbling stream to wash her face and greet the morning.

After a filling breakfast of hot herbal tea, orange juice, porridge and buckwheat griddle cakes cooked on a flat stone, for all except Carol, who insisted on a bowl of Froot Loops® and a cheese danish, the plucky band washed their dishes and policed the area, taking special care to dismantle the lean-to and extinguish the fire, spreading the ashes around to circumvent their reigniting themselves. When they had finished these chores and put the dishes and leftovers back in the mystic inner pocket of Eve's cloak, Eve called the girls together and assembled everyone at the bottom step of the stile.

"Remember what Santa warned us about 'The Fade' and the dangers we might face there, girls!" cautioned Eve. "Stay together as a group and don't accept anything you see at face value."

"We won't," chirped Holly.

"Don't worry, Eve, I'll keep these two in line!" barked Noel.

"Can I get Elvis's autograph?" queried Carol.

Having given her last minute admonition, Christmas Eve started up the steps to the stile. As she traversed the top step, she began to fade from sight like a lifting fog at daybreak. Stifling their

amazement, the Sugar Plum Fairies flitted after the rapidly vanish-
ing form of their friend, growing more transparent themselves until,
scant moments later, all four figures were gone from the natural
world. The wind played harshly across the rickety steps, blowing
and swirling powdery snow in its wake as tree branches rustled
and creaked in the breeze. Far in the distance, a forlorn crow
cawed out his loneliness, but no other sound was heard. Christmas
Eve, Holly, Noel and Carol had entered The Fade.

The journey into The Fade was simple enough; like stepping over
the threshold from one room to the next. There were a few flashes
of light… magenta, then amber, then magenta again, accompanied
by a soothing, melodious trilling, like one might hear played on a
piccolo. Dry, dusty voices whispered the secrets of the universe
into their ears, reverberating through the air in barely audible tones.
An abrupt blast of warm air assaulted the travelers, then suddenly
it was all over.

Christmas Eve and the Sugar Plum Fairies were standing amidst
lush tropical foliage where mere seconds before all was barren
arctic tundra. Butterflies and rabbits fluttered and scampered
through gardens of flowers, impressive with vibrant colors and
senses-satisfying aromas. In the distance, they could see a jade-
dappled dell, with fruit trees and soft, undulating emerald grass. In
the center of the dell was a tranquil, mirror-smooth pool with a
smallish waterfall at the far end. Dragonflies and frogs buzzed and
cavorted among the reeds and lily pads nestled along the far shore
midst the white spray foam from the waterfall. Around the lake pad-
dled a magnificent trumpeter swan, its white feathers aflame with
dazzling ivory magnificence. Eve and the girls drank in the resplendent beauty, filling their senses with the sights, sounds and smells.

"This place ROCKS!" exclaimed Noel, barely containing her exu-
berance.

"Being here is almost as good as getting a puppy on Christmas
morning," remarked Holly, trying to retain some measure of

decorum.

"Gooder-er!" squealed Carol as she ran in circles on the verdant lawn, "Can we play here awhile, Christmas Eve?"

"That's a fine idea, Carol," replied Eve, "it'll give us a chance to get our bearings. You girls enjoy yourselves, but be careful! I'll be down by that pond."

Eve carefully made her way to the shimmering pool. Along the way, she paused to remove her boots, allowing the dew bejeweled grass to tickle her toes. When she reached the near shore of the pond, Eve removed her cape and spread it out like a picnic blanket on the mossy bank. Looking back to ascertain the girls' safety, she giggled amiably at the sight of Holly and Noel, beneath leafy fruit trees, picking apples and plums off the ground and Carol chasing butterflies. With the girls safe at play, Eve stretched out on the cape, warming herself in the dappled sunlight and casually splashing her toes in the cool, inviting lake water.

Holly and Noel turned their attention from fruit gathering to playing with the small native fauna. While they romped with the bunnies and squirrels, Carol was, in her turn, being chased by the very butterflies she had pursued moments earlier. Eve continued to soak in the tranquility of their surroundings as the swan swam closer to shore, reassured that the intruders meant it no harm. As the swan weaved to and fro across the lake, drawing ever closer to shore, Eve began softly humming a catchy tune, part "Jingle Bells", part made up melody. The soft, rhythmic splashing of her toes in the water attracted the swan ever nearer. After a few moments, the swan began gliding back and forth in front of Eve, swaying its neck from side to side in an almost hypnotic pattern. In the midst of all the pleasurable sights and sounds that engulfed her, Christmas Eve grew drowsy and serene. The swan playfully began nibbling Eve's toes. Eve tittered approvingly. The swan, now completely at ease with the stranger, began nuzzling Eve's ankles.

The swan had made its way no more than an inch up her leg, however, when Eve suddenly sat bolt upright and with a lightning fast lunge, grasped the swan firmly around the neck and wouldn't let go. The swan began frantically flapping its wings and honking hysterically, hoping its twisting gyrations would induce Eve to loosen her grip. By this time, the Sugar Plum Fairies, alerted and alarmed by the swan's violent struggling, had reached the shore, stunned by their friend's seemingly casual cruelty.

"Eve! What are you doing?" screeched Holly.

"Did he bite you or what?" question Noel.

"Oh, that poor birdie!" yowled Carol.

Despite their protestations, however, Eve refused to loosen her grip, actually seeming to tighten it the more the swan thrashed about. Finally, seeming to come to grips with its predicament, the swan resignedly ceased its struggles, becoming limp in Eve's vice like grasp. When Eve was certain that the swan was finished with its antics, she lifted the harried bird to her eye level, staring down the vanquished waterfowl with a flinty gaze. As the swan watched, helpless, a sly, triumphant sardonic smile passed across Eve's lips.

"Hello… Zeus," chirped Christmas Eve.

END CHAPTER THREE

Chapter Four

The previously tranquil glade suddenly became a beehive of activity and confusion. The Sugar Plum Fairies swooped about Christmas Eve in a frantic, frenetic flight pattern as the swan, seeming to catch a second breath, began its frenzied maneuverings anew. As the bird's hectic struggling grew more intense, the very air surrounding it and Eve began to shimmer with scintillating flashes of pure white light.

"That's not a swan… it's an alligator!" wept Holly.

Surely enough, Eve was now grasping a large bayou alligator tightly by its gullet, holding firm despite the beast's flashing claws, flailing tail and razor sharp, snapping teeth.

"No! It… it's a 'AMACONGA..!'" bawled Carol as she flew off behind a bush, covering her eyes in fear of the huge carnivorous reptile.

Eve now found herself holding a massive, undulating snake, an anaconda, by the throat. It coiled tighter about her forearms, unhinging its massive serpentine jaw with the intent of swallowing the Christmas super heroine whole. Eve stood unyielding before the maw of certain doom.

"Whoa! Looka the size of that bear!" howled Noel.

Eve staunchly maintained her vise-like grip on the esophagus of the now ursine terror. Amidst the frightful roars and thrashing of colossal paws, Christmas Eve simply smiled and tightened her grip ever so slightly around the wind pipe of her metamorphic opponent, causing him/it to choke and gasp for air.

"I can keep this up as long as you can, thunder god," jibed Eve.

Suddenly, all machinations ceased and the bear, now in the man-like form of Zeus, surrendered to Eve.

"I yield, fair one! Release your grip and you'll have no further trouble from me. So swears Zeus, ruler of Olympus."

Eve slackened her grip and stood, waiting, while Zeus caught his breath, massaging his neck in wincing, obvious discomfort. The three fairies hovered nearby in amazement at the Greek deity's ability to change form, seemingly at will.

"Ooh! Be a unicorn, Mr. Zeus!" twittered Holly.

"No! A dragon!" bellowed Noel, showing clawed hands and huffing out imaginary fire.

"A beanbag chair!" interjected Carol.

"Girls! Hush!" came Eve's exasperated reply. "What's this all about, Mr. Zeus? Why'd you attack us?"

"I..? I attack YOU..? I was about nuzzling your ankles, madam! T'was YOU who assaulted ME!" sputtered Zeus indignantly.

"Fair enough, I suppose," acquiesced Eve, "But why were you nuzzling my ankles..?" Eve had barely gotten the words out when a voice like steel wool wrapped in honey chimed in from behind them.

"It's just something the old reprobate does from time to time. I thought we'd cured him of that particularly nasty practice some years ago but, apparently, old habits die hard on the slopes of Olympus."

They turned, with wonderment on their faces (and more than a little fear in the eyes of Zeus) to behold Hera, Queen of Mount Olympus and Zeus's wife. Hera stood next to a gold and pearl chariot, fronted by two snow white stallions, just beneath the first few fruit trees in the dappled glen. Her eyes burned with a strict disciplinary fire, reserved solely for Zeus.

"I'll settle with you when we return home, lecherous worm," Hera spat at Zeus, "But…" she continued, softening her demeanor but maintaining a regal air, "since my husband seems quite incapable of conducting the proper business of The Fade that he is charged with, it falls to me to ask what brings you four to trespass at the gates of our realm?"

Eve, showing the proper etiquette when addressing royalty, began to explain their purpose for venturing into The Fade but was cut abruptly short by Hera's regal upraised hand.

"This seems a longish tale best told in the pillowed halls of the Olympian palace, where sweet fruit nectar flows freely and Feta cheese and bread are always in abundance…"

With that, Hera beckoned Eve and the girls to board her glorious chariot as she took up the reins and prepared to urge her steeds into a full gallop. Just before she gave the command, however, she turned sternly towards her wayward husband.

"You, sir, I believe, shall walk home! And know, O' mighty Zeus, that I am fully aware the length of time it takes to scale the heathered slopes of Olympus and should expect you not one moment later than that span of hours."

With that rebuke, Hera cracked her whip and she, Christmas Eve and the Sugar Plum Fairies were off, leaving a contrite and humbled Zeus alone amidst a cloud of dust to choke out a grumbled "yes, dear".

When Zeus finally arrived at the palace, Hera, Eve and the girls were carrying on like school girls on a weekend sleepover. The chief god hoped that the laughter and song coming from the throne room meant that the hours it took for him to hike home had softened Hera's heart, making the arduous trek well worth the effort. The instantaneous deafening silence and flinty gaze from his better half as he entered through the portico put the lie to that notion almost immediately. Slinking remorsefully to his throne, Zeus mumbled several epithets beneath his breath usually spoken by only the doughtiest of seamen.

"Beg pardon, my husband?" smirked Hera.

"I simply said, my love," oiled Zeus in a faux innocence, "I'm sure my darling Hera, most beauteous of all the goddesses in fair Olympus, more exquisite than the dazzling penumbra of the new moon, envy of the sunrise and covetous ideal for the midsummer's morning dew has by now employed her insightful wits and rapier sharp intelligence in ascertaining the purpose of our 'guests'… none of whom holds the slightest interest for me, mind you… in darkening our doorway uninvited and most certainly unbidden."

"Indeed I have, sire!" warbled Hera with a smile, as she turned her back on the ruler of Olympus and proceeded to re-engage Christmas Eve and her coterie of fairies in girlish small talk of fashion and make-up tips.

Zeus slumped deep into his chair, resting his head heavily on his right hand, elbow cocked in a most blasé manner. His left hand fingers drummed out an impatient tattoo on the throne's marble armrest which belied his feigned nonchalance. This continued for several minutes which, to Zeus, seemed longer even than his uphill trudge back to Olympus from the dappled dell.

"Well..?" he barked finally.

"'Well' what, dearest?" came the queen of the gods good natured reply.

"Well," continued the visibly exasperated monarch, "has my wife discerned the reason for our visitors' untimely call? If so, perhaps the queen of my heart might deign to share this acquired knowledge with the room..?"

"As you wish, my liege," retorted Hera mischievously.

After Hera and Christmas Eve told Zeus all about Santa's plight and the heinous theft of the Golden Garland, with many descriptive interjections about Charlie The Yeti and the nature of Yetis in general by the girls, the supreme monarch of Olympus wasted no time in convening his court to consider what their next action might be.

Reactions and suggestions were varied. Herakles, the Greek representation of fabled Hercules and Zeus's son, wanted to pound someone, anyone, into paste. Not surprisingly, this plan was summarily dismissed, allowing that this was Herakles' solution to almost EVERY problem. Aphrodite, goddess of love, suggested that perhaps if the Yetis were approached with arms opened in an aspect of brotherly love all would be made well. Carol supported that plan wholeheartedly, but the general approval for this notion throughout the court waned when the discussions devolved into Carol, Aphrodite and Pan the Satyr holding hands and singing "Kumbayah". Hermes, the swift, wing-footed messenger of the gods was no help at all. He just ran willy-nilly around the throne room, flitting hither and yon. Watching him made Noel sort of queasy. Finally, Hephaestus posited the idea of simply making a NEW Golden Garland strand for Eve to take back to Santa.

"O' wretched dwarf!" bellowed Zeus, "Your addled brain has become as warped as your twisted form! To replace the garland in such a common manner only serves to cheapen the sentiment of the original and debases our heartfelt tribute to the One God, Creator of All That Is!"

"Now, now, my lord," cooed Hera, "Hephaestus was only offering a suggestion. We're all looking for a proper solution. No need to get testy."

Regardless of his unseemly outburst and Hera's chiding, Zeus was essentially correct thought Eve and, as the deliberations continued, the First Lady of Yuletide Cheer watched with awe the manner in which Hera guided the conversation and totally controlled her husband's mercurial temperament. She was beginning to see the wisdom in Santa's choice of her as his ambassador to The Fade. The dynamic was plain. She and Hera got along famously and Hera, of course, was the true power behind the throne. Hera, however, probably would not have gone against her husband on matters of state under normal conditions. But Eve's obvious charms coupled with Zeus' licentious nature provided just the impetus that Hera needed to take charge, with Zeus behaving much too subserviently to countermand her.

"Santa truly does know who's naughty or nice… even Zeus", chuckled Eve to herself.

Her reverie was cut short when Zeus rose and held forth his scepter. A proclamation from the Greek thunder god was imminent and everyone gathered pricked up their ears in anticipation. Pausing to allow the room to fully come to attention (and, admittedly, for regal effect), Zeus held his chin aloft, flared his nostrils and started his oration.

"The situation before us is one that requires much thought and decisive action. Though I speak for the general welfare of all denizens of The Fade, I may not infringe on any of the other kingdoms' autonomy," Zeus began.

"Further, though this theft is not the fault of Santa Claus, alerting the other monarchies to the Golden Garland's pilferage would only serve to incite and enrage those less cultured than ourselves…"

Herakles snorted derisively. Zeus scowled at his son with contempt, then continued.

"As I said, such action would only serve to bring contempt to Saint Nicholas' seemingly cavalier handling of our great gift and I am loathe to subject our dear friend to that sort of undeserved resentment. So, therefore, it is the ruling of this august body that Christmas Eve and her cadre of Sugar Plum Fairies be allowed free passage across all regions of The Fade…"

Eve and the girls were riveted to their seats, now. Zeus was coming to the crux of his speech. What was expected of them in order for them to complete their mission and, more importantly, what sort of help could they expect from the lord of Olympus? Zeus spoke on.

"But this passage must be made furtively, with cautious stealth, throughout the different realms in search of Charlie The Yeti… and ONLY for the express purpose of returning the Golden Garland to Santa Claus and bringing Charlie The Yeti to a swift and sure justice. "

So far, so good, thought Christmas Eve. She and the Sugar Plum Fairies had no other agenda in their visit to The Fade. Their every intention was just as Zeus outlined. But what of mighty Olympus? What role would this jeweled realm play in facilitating Eve's search? Zeus cleared his throat. This was it. The anticipation in the throne room was palpable.

"As for we of fabled Olympus, in our infinite wisdom, have decided as a group to do… NOTHING!"

"O' Holy Night!" exclaimed Eve.

END CHAPTER FOUR

Chapter Five

Henry Cobbler quite liked Christmas, actually. That was not an easy thing for a Druid-in-training to say aloud, especially one attending Stonehenge Academy for the first time. But Henry had been raised in an orphanage in Lancastershire by normal Britons, far removed from his heritage as a Druid. Every year, St. Augustus' Orphanage had a Christmas tree and the staff made sure that each child living there got something in their stocking. On Christmas Day, the town's local charitable institutions supplied a Christmas turkey dinner for the orphans and Christmas afternoon was an endless parade of carol singing, laughter, gift opening and gorging on Figgie pudding and sweets. Henry enjoyed everything about the holiday and never gave a thought to how a true Druid looked at these activities.

The Druids, as a whole, were quite bitter about the entire Christmas season. The Winter Solstice celebration was a special time for all Druids and they didn't take kindly to their "high holy days" being co-opted by the Christians lo, those many centuries ago. Sharing their special time with another religion wasn't so bad in and of itself. However, over the centuries, Christmas became more and more worldly until, now, the whole world celebrates it whether they believe in anything in particular or not and the root druidic meanings of the mid-winter festival have become lost to the ages. The Druids had been edged out of their own holiday. This engendered much ill will amongst the druidic community and their greatest rancor was reserved for the single most popular symbol of that

Christmas co-opt… Santa Claus, or Father Christmas as he was called in Henry Cobbler's village. But, the Druids had long ago relocated to The Fade and turned their backs on the world of normal men, or "Celtlings", as they were derisively nicknamed at Stonehenge Academy, and had happily gone back to celebrating the Winter Solstice in their own manner, yet still harboring their bitterness towards Santa, a bitterness that they passed down from generation to generation, instilling their disdain for all things Christmas into their children from birth. Henry Cobbler, though, was raised amongst the Celtlings and had no such bias.

So, Henry Cobbler kept his love of Christmas to himself and concentrated on his druidic studies, not wishing to feel anymore the outsider than he already was. In fact, in a school of several hundred Druids, teachers and staff, Henry, a bespectacled bookwormish sort, only had two real friends, Ferret Reynolds and Guinevere Upington-Smythe.

"Wot's all this, then 'Enry Cobbler?" commented Ferret Reynolds, breezing into their shared dorm, freckle-faced and uncombed, "'Ow can you study at a time like this? 'Aven't you 'eard? The 'Eadmaster saw a bloomin' Yeti skulking around the campus night before last an' Custodian Homberg 'as offered a tidy tuppence for 'is capture to put in the school's menagerie! Oi'm fancyin' a right proper Yeti safari, Oi am! Come along, 'Enry..!"

Despite his casual manner, Ferret Reynolds could be quite persuasive if given half a chance and, after much wheedling, he convinced Henry to accompany him on their grand adventure into the world of bounty hunting. After gathering up such tools as they deemed necessary to perform the stalker's art, they slunk down a darkened corridor that led indirectly to the quad, taking special pains not to arouse anyone's curiosity. They had almost made it to the greensward when their worst fears became reality. A voice like shaved ice on a hot August day cut the air, halting the two boys dead in their tracks.

"Lord love a duck, where are you two ne'er-do-wells off to, then?" came the voice from behind, tinged with self-importance and fairly dripping with condescension.

This was Guinevere Upington-Smythe. She was a classmate of
Henry and Ferret's who lived over in the girl's dormitory. Guinevere
was a prissy little know-it-all who took a shine to the two wayward
boys the first day she met them on the back of the oxcart that was
taking them all to The Fade entrance to Stonehenge Academy. No
one knows why Guinevere is chums with the boys. Some say that
her pomposity is off putting and no one else at the academy wants
to be her friend. Others assume that she likes the company of
Henry and, especially, Ferret because she really doesn't have to try
all that hard to feel superior to either of them. Whatever the reason,
Henry and Ferret both look upon Guinevere as a circumstantial ally
at best.

"Hello, Guinevere," the boys moaned in unison.

"We're off on an adventure," offered Henry, "We fancy ourselves
bounty hunters today."

"Yah! And no girls allowed!" snapped Ferret.

"And where might this bounty of yours be found, wot?" questioned Guinevere.

"We don't rightly know," said Henry, "We just thought we'd start
looking down by the old haunted grist mill beyond the south lawn.
Care to join us?"

"Cor, 'Enry! We don't need no flippin' birds 'angin' all over us,
then!" protested Ferret.

"I'd love to accompany you, Henry Cobbler!" Guinevere squealed
with delight.

After a few more uncomfortable moments and dirty looks between Ferret and Guinevere, the trio was off for the haunted grist
mill, their poke laden with spell candles, silver bells, a ceremonial
rubber dagger, a yo-yo, several head cheese sandwiches, a length

of rope, a sprig of mistletoe and other sundry tools of the bounty hunter's trade.

"Where'd you get that scar on your forehead, Henry," asked Guinevere?

"Ferret hauled off one day and hit me with a cricket bat," replied Henry, not breaking stride.

"Rubbish and rot! It were an accident, for sure, 'Enry Cobbler!" objected Ferret.

"Was not!"

"Was so!"

"Not!"

"So!"

Guinevere wondered exactly how far away the old haunted grist mill was and if there wasn't some sort of magical druidic incantation that could get them there that much quicker.

Christmas Eve stood shocked at Zeus' proclamation. She was hoping for perhaps some small effort on the part of the Olympians to assist her and the girls in their search. She was formulating a reply to the declaration, running the words over and over in her mind, trying to find the exact right thing to say that would both register her displeasure with the ruling yet not insult the mercurial ruler, when Hera stood up and demanded the floor.

"Erase the furrows from thy brow, my sweet Christmas Eve," chuckled Hera, "We have every intention of helping you to the best of our abilities. We simply must strive to avoid conflict with the other domains within The Fade. As such, we Olympians cannot venture throughout the land in force, trampling with impunity on the property rights of our brethren! No, we must remain here and give off the impression of impartiality at the very least."

"Then how are you to help us, O' Queen?" queried Eve.

"Good question, Eve!" replied Holly.

"Yeah! Good one!" echoed Noel.

"Can we sing 'Kumbayah' again?" asked Carol, "I really like that song".

"In addition to our sincerest well wishes and hope for your success, we offer you these gifts," continued Hera, "A map of The Fade, similar to the one we granted Santa Claus, that indicates all the entrance and exit points in each territory and a bronze ring with a compass mounted in it that contains a golden needle, fashioned by Hephaestus from the same gold used in creating the Golden Garland, that always points in the direction of the Garland. With these travel aids at your disposal, you should have little trouble locating your quarry."

"Thank you, great Hera," responded Christmas Eve with a polite curtsy.

"May the winds of Zephyrus provide you swift passage on your journey, Yuletide Defender!" answered Hera back with much obvious affection.

"We are adjourned!" roared Zeus, flinching slightly and casting a sheepish glance in Hera's direction, looking for some small sign of approbation. Hera nodded and smiled at her husband, encouraging him to regain his regal comportment.

Christmas Eve and her companions flew at a rapid clip until Olympus was no more than a speck on the horizon before they lit in a dense forest to consult their map, eat some lunch and get a heading from the compass ring.

"C'n I have a ham sammich?" asked Noel, "I really didn't like that stinky fetid cheese they had on Olympus."

"It's pronounced 'feta' cheese," corrected Holly.

"With a smell like that, it's 'fetid'," quipped Noel.

Eve produced a hearty, healthful lunch of baked ham and Colby Jack cheese on whole wheat sandwiches, carrot sticks, almonds, juice boxes and fruit cups from her marvelous cape's pouch. While they ate on the ground, picnic style, Eve carefully unfolded the map and, holding the compass ring aloft, ran her index finger over the map, tracing along in the direction the compass needle was pointing, attempting to plot their course.

"Charlie seems to be moving in a northwesterly direction, from the Himalayas, through Asia to the Germanic regions," mused Eve.

"Eve, why would Charlie steal something at the North Pole then go half a world away only to head back in the direction he started from?" asked Holly.

"Maybe he got losted," offered Carol, "Yetis aren't very bright."

"You got that right, sister!" retorted Noel.

"Girls! That's not very nice! True, but not nice," scolded Eve, "Still, who really knows what goes on in the mind of a Yeti, especially one as contrary as Charlie apparently is. In any event, it looks like we're heading northwest… to England."

END CHAPTER FIVE

Chapter Six

Nobody in his village ever cared much for Charlie and he cared even less for them. Ever since he'd been a cub, the other Yeti cubs tormented him. No one quite knew why Charlie was the butt of everyone's taunting, not even the elders in the Council of Free Yetis. That's just the way it always had been and, it seemed, always would be. It's no wonder then that Charlie kept to himself in a small grotto on the north face of Bittercold Mountain.

Over the years, as Charlie grew meaner, more sullen and more withdrawn, his hermitic lifestyle gave rise to many urban legends among the Yeti wives and Charlie became somewhat of a mysterious "boogeyman", whose name was invoked to keep the Yeti cubs in line, causing Charlie's resentment and the villagers' fear to increase day by day. It was said that the only Yeti who seemed to have any affection for Charlie at all was his Uncle Grimfang from the "old country" in Tibet.

The Himalayan Yetis, like their North American cousins, the Sasquatches, had long since moved their society into the nurturing confines of The Fade. The North Pole Yetis, due mostly to the relative seclusion of living so near Christmas Valley, had not. This made contact between the two tribes difficult, but Uncle Grimfang wrote to Charlie often, regaling him with tales of starting avalanches and burying Mongol warriors beneath tons of ice and sharing family recipes for Mountain Antelope Stew. Charlie, for his part, always sent Uncle Grimfang a Christmas present from the swag he collected during the Yetis annual December pilgrimage to Santa's Village looking for handouts, although most of Charlie's loot was gathered from raids on his own village.

Charlie would crouch outside the school barrow, where he would yowl a mournful wail and frighten the Yeti cubs into dropping their goodies and scampering for their home caves. Sometimes, though, Charlie would join the march into Santa's Village. Charlie HATED this. The bright twinkly lights, the warm, cozy dwellings, the pervasive joy and the happy smiling faces of the elves reminded Charlie of everything his own wretched life was not and this filled him with an almost tangible rage. Someday, Charlie thought, he would wreck his vengeance on Santa's entire Christmas Empire. It was on one of these infrequent trips into Santa's Village that Charlie first heard tell of the Golden Garland of Zeus.

"Perfect," snarled Charlie under his breath, "I can bring this whole operation to a screeching halt and, using the Garland for its intended purpose, travel freely through The Fade to visit my Uncle Grimfang! What wonderful tales of holiday mischief we will share then!"

So, one icy, moonless night in mid-December, Charlie stole into Santa's Workshop and Stables and made off with the Golden Garland of Zeus. Making his way to the hidden stile next to the rill just beyond the copse of evergreens, Charlie vanished from our world into The Fade, with only the echo of his coarse, maniacal laughter remaining as evidence he'd ever been there at all.

Unlike Christmas Eve and the girls, Charlie did not emerge in the dappled glen in the shadow of Mount Olympus when he entered The Fade. Rather, the apelike humanoid found himself on a night-dark cobblestone Parisian boulevard. As he was getting his bearings, Charlie heard the steely clip clop of galloping horses' hooves and shouting French accented voices. He turned to see three leather clad men brandishing swords.

"Do not move, mon ami! In the name of our most regal monarch,

King Louis XIII, you are in the custody of The Three Musketeers!" came the voice of Athos, captain of the king's Musketeers. Charlie was amazed that he could understand French, but chalked it up to the magic of The Fade.

Charlie began tensing his powerful leg muscles and flexing his clawed hands in an effort to spring on his captors in feral savagery before they knew what hit them. He was feeling cranky and spoiling for a fight, a whim, he reckoned to himself, these fools would so conveniently oblige. Swords and muskets drawn, the Musketeers dismounted warily, never taking their collective eyes off their hirsute prisoner. It seemed as though Charlie would get his wish when one of them noticed the Golden Garland tucked loosely in the top of Charlie's lederhosen.

"Mon dieu, mes amis! He has the Golden Garland of Zeus in his possession! Surely he is an emissary of Pere Noel!" exclaimed Porthos, the second Musketeer.

"Um… yeah… we'll go with that," snarled Charlie, "Season's Greetings and like that! Now, what seems to be the problem, officers?"

Charlie wasn't very good at thinking on the fly, but he was a masterful liar. The Musketeer's obvious reverence for the Golden Garland left him torn. He could parlay the situation into his advantage, gaining directions, free passage, maybe some food and transportation, but he sure would hate to miss a good fight. Finally, after what seemed like an eternity, his more pragmatic nature won out. Charlie decided to lie through his pointed teeth.

"We are most sorry, mon ami!" apologized Aramis, the third Musketeer, "We did not notice the Golden Garland in the sparse light of this darkened street. We have pledged to honor the ruling from the Great Santa Claus Trial and offer all due hospitality to the bearer of the aureate swag. How may we assist you?"

"I'm on my way to Tibet," lied Charlie, "To, uh, build a runway, yeah… a runway… for Santa to land his team on for, um… a lunch break. Anyway, I need directions, maybe some food and, um… a horse?"

"Mes oui, mon frere! We are most pleased to provide a map to one of Pere Noel's agents! And food, ah, our French food is beyond compare! We invite you to join us at our favorite inn… the victuals are, how you say, on the house!" effused Athos.

"Sadly, though," interjected Porthos, "We are forbidden to allow one of our steeds to traverse outside the confines of our territory within The Fade. Such an act would violate all manner of treaties!"

"But we would be most pleased to provide a mount and escort you to the border," offered Aramis.

"Yeah, okay," stammered Charlie, carefully building his rapidly growing mountain of lies and trying not to show his obvious disappointment in not copping a free ride, "Let's go eat and hit the road, um… toot sweet!"

Less than three hours later, well fed and mellow from numerous flagons of ale, Charlie dismounted at the border of the Musketeer's legendary Renaissance France. For a moment, he entertained the notion of turning on his hosts and, after a gloriously bloody battle, just taking the horse, but he was far too logy from imbibing the splendid French wine to give the idea serious consideration. Instead, Charlie The Yeti gruffly thanked his escort, bowed clumsily, and staggered across the border on foot. As the riders urged their mounts homeward and disappeared over the horizon, Charlie, his head starting to clear a little in the cool night air, began to earnestly search for the pass indicated on his map that led through the Carpathian Mountains to the tiny country of Transylvania.

Henry Cobbler was smitten. The odd feeling had been churning about in his stomach for several weeks but he dismissed it as either a mild case of the flu or indigestion from filching one too many blood sausages with Ferret on one of their midnight raids on the dormitory pantry. The true cause of his nausea had only begun to dawn on him within the last two or three days when, he noticed his abdominal cramps only manifested themselves when Guinevere Upington-Smythe was around.

How could such a thing have happened to him thought Henry; and with HER, of all people? Guinevere was the most annoying person he'd ever met, even for a girl. She was bossy, conceited, condescending and downright rude. Still, Henry mused, she displayed a certain grace of movement and her voice, though domineering, had a trilling lilt to it that very much pleased Henry's ears. Plus, too, she smelled really, really nice despite being daily surrounded by the many noxious fumes that accompanied their potion-making in Conjuration 101. As the trio of "bounty hunters" made their way over the wildflower bedecked hills, down through a rocky ravine that led to the lazy stream that flowed past the old, haunted gristmill, Henry found his gaze frequently falling on Guinevere's cascading golden hair, windblown and free, playing casually across her porcelain cheeks and soft, strawberry lips. This distraction caused him to stumble much more than usual for a gangly boy of fifteen.

"First day with the new feet, is it, Henry?" mocked Guinevere. Her remarks were casually cruel and she scoffed at his embarrassment. Henry didn't seem to mind.

"Roight, then, 'ere we are" whispered Ferret Reynolds, pushing aside some bramble bushes to reveal the ramshackle shed, "H'it's stealth from 'ere on or Bob's your uncle!"

"Are you coming, then, 'Enry Cobbler?" asked Ferret over his shoulder as he made his way down the rise, on his stomach in a serpentine crawl, a length of rope in his ruddy fist, "We 'ave to set a proper snare for the Yeti over by that grove of trees."

"You go on ahead, Ferret, " motioned Henry, drawing furtively closer to Guinevere, "We'll go down to the stream by the mill's water wheel and sit guard, hidden in that clump of tall grass and reeds by the river bank."

Ferret spat in disgust and kept crawling. Guinevere giggled and looked at Henry with an impish twinkle in her sapphire blue eyes. Yes, Henry Cobbler was smitten.

Christmas Eve and her Sugar Plum companions landed clandestinely on a sloping terra cotta tiled roof in a Victorian England-style section of The Fade. At least that's how it seemed. The Fade was a patchwork hodge-podge of different eras and characteristics, nestled tightly alongside one another. Though the section of town the four companions now found themselves in was, without a doubt, Victorian, they could see rolling countryside dotted with serfdoms clustered about a walled castle high atop a hill off in the distance that looked to be of Middle Ages design.

As they regained their bearings, giving the Sugar Plums a short break to stretch their wings and shake off a little fairy dust, Eve let her mind wander back to the people, places and things they'd seen since leaving Olympus. The Fade was a truly wondrous and frightening place, with much beauty and equal amounts of peril. They had had to travel slowly, cautiously and deliberately, not having the benefit of possessing the Golden Garland to grant them free travel throughout The Fade. Still, in spite of their constant danger, the four of them experienced some remarkable events and met some genuinely pleasant people.

Their first stop after departing the Olympian Greek Isle was the Italian mainland, where they exchanged pasta recipes with Marco Polo and helped Christopher Columbus repair a hole in the hull of the Santa Maria. Moving inland, they spent some time stargazing with Galileo, who even promised to name a star after Holly. The Fade didn't discriminate between actual persons and literary or fanciful creations either, as evidenced by Carol exchanging knock-knock jokes with Pagliacci. You only had to achieve some manner of legendary status, it seemed, to become a resident of The Fade.

Traveling northwest, the friends met Don Quixote, who helped them avoid entanglements with Tomás de Torquemada and the dread Spanish Inquisition, whose strict orthodoxy would not have allowed for fairies or Eve's brand of Christmas symbolism. Circumventing the Inquisition, however, resulted in the hardy travelers detouring through Germany, where they wound up in a pitched aerial battle with the Flying Circus, led by Baron Manfred von Richthofen. The fairies frenzied flitting and Eve's graceful aerial acrobatics notwithstanding, the Red Baron had them dead to rights, save for the last minute assistance of an American flyer who, in the blazing, smoke-filled murk over occupied Europe, looked conspicuously like a small dog.

Eventually reaching France, Christmas Eve, Holly, Noel and Carol met up with The Musketeers who, when Eve explained to them about Charlie and the theft of the Garland, were regretful for their part in the caper and gave the foursome an armed escort to the banks of the English Channel, where they were smuggled across the channel by Sir Percy Blakeney in his guise as the Scarlet Pimpernel, who likened their quest to his own endeavors, intoning "you seek him here, you seek him there, you seek that Yeti everywhere!" This made Carol giggle uncontrollably all the way across the channel.

Eve's reverie was sharply interrupted by a hysterical caterwauling coming from the cobbled alley below the roof she was resting on. The girls had fluttered down to the ground to take a quick look at the quaint houses and shops that occupied this tract of The Fade's London and now were being chased by an immense, slavering bull mastiff.

END CHAPTER SIX

Chapter Seven

Charlie The Yeti, regardless of the animosity heaped on him for most of his misbegotten life, had never before been chased by villagers with torches and pitchforks and he did not like it one little bit! How he came to such mean consequences was a bewilderment to the eight foot tall Yeti, but there it was. He pondered the dire turn of events that led to his predicament as he raced through the Transylvanian darkness.

With the Golden Garland of Zeus securely in his possession, Charlie had no difficulty making his way from Renaissance France into the foothills of the Carpathian Mountains. Even as he climbed further up the slopes, sneakily passing dreary little hamlets and detouring around the occasional Gypsy encampment, it was relatively easy going for the hairy man-brute. Once he reached the ravine that was the start of the mountain pass, Charlie thought the rest of his trip through the mountains would be smooth sailing. Not so.

After Charlie had been traveling for some hours, winding his way up and down one craggy path after another, he came to a tiny village huddled next to a sheer cliff face. The village was markedly gloomy, fairly swallowed up by unnaturally murky shadows, most of which were cast by an imposing citadel hewn out of the top of the rock face. The stone fortress reeked of evil but, being rather malicious himself, Charlie paid scant heed to it. Charlie's only concern was reaching the Himalayas and Uncle Grimfang by the shortest route possible. As he peered, squinting through the gloom, at the town square, his red eyes scanned the stables and sheds hoping, perhaps, to appropriate a horse-drawn hay wagon or an ox-driven cart or even a donkey, anything that would save him from walking all the way to Tibet.

As he was about to step out of the deep darkness he was currently skulking in, however, Charlie felt an unseen hand grasp him tightly about the shoulder and yank him harshly back into the gloomy alleyway, spinning him around and slamming his back roughly against the shadowed stone wall of a peasant hovel. Charlie was momentarily stunned, the unexpected action knocking the wind out of his massive frame. As his vision cleared and his eyes grew accustomed to the dim light, he noticed that the unseen hand had grown no more visible in the intervening seconds. All that stood in front of him was an overcoat, trousers, a fedora and dark glasses. With no discernable head or torso to hold them up, the accouterments appeared to be floating in mid-air in front of Charlie.

"Edward, you old scalawag," whispered the Invisible Man, "What are you doing here? Victor sent me out to meet Henry".

"Henry?" repeated Charlie.

"Yes. Henry Jekyll! Don't play coy with me, old boy! I can see right through you," chided the Invisible Man.

"Whoa! Hold on, pal! You have the wrong guy! I'm just…" started Charlie.

Then, in an uncharacteristic moment of clarity, Charlie began thinking how it had been many hours since his last meal back at the French roadside inn and how, maybe, his unseen assailant might just be able to provide some grub if Charlie played his cards right.

"…um, like you said, trying to get to Victor's," continued Charlie clumsily, "Good old Victor! And such a wonderful cook, too! Lead on, pal!"

Charlie hoped his lie was convincing but it was pretty hard to read a guy with no visible head. Still, the Invisible Man made no protestation but simply turned and motioned with an empty sleeve for Charlie to follow him.

Come, then, friend Hyde," offered Charlie's vanished guide with a wry chortle, "To the castle laboratory and 'good old Victor'".

The castle atop the mountain was cold and dank and its chiseled granite steps were slippery and caked with moss. The blackened, pitch covered torches that lined the wall sputtered and burned dimly, giving off plumes of dark acrid smoke. They were met at the main door by a weird little hunchback with a wandering eye who merely grunted, turned and led them down a long cobweb infested corridor towards a door marked "laboratory".

"Victor should have everything set up by now, Edward," mentioned the Invisible Man, "Shouldn't you begin your transformation back to Henry Jekyll?"

"Before dinner?" questioned Charlie, his stomach growling. He wasn't sure who this Henry Jekyll was, or Edward Hyde, for that matter, but Charlie's only interest was in securing a hot meal and getting gone. If that meant he had to pretend to be Hyde, then so be it, but he wanted his meal first, before anyone saw through his clever (to him, anyway) masquerade.

"Don't spar with me, Edward, I'm not in the mood," snarled Charlie's indiscernible cohort, "Victor feels a combination of his and your specialized scientific backgrounds may afford a cure for my debilitating skin condition and I mean to have it sooner rather than later!"

"Skin condition?" inquired Charlie, completely bewildered.

"Yes. My skin… you can't see it..! A most intolerable condition!" laughed the Invisible Man.

The peculiar little hunchback paused before the great oaken door to the lab, gestured towards the knob, grunted something neither Charlie nor his undetectable friend could quite understand then scampered off down the passageway into the arms of the enveloping darkness. An invisible hand slowly turned the large brass knob and gingerly opened the door, the hinges creaking a dour, mournful dirge. When the two entered the lab, they were at once taken aback by the intense brightness of the crackling electric glow emanating from the numerous banks of elaborately arcane machinery lining every wall. As their vision adjusted to the mechanical dazzle before them, Charlie began gazing about the laboratory for a buffet table or a pastry cart or something. The Invisible Man's gaze was riveted elsewhere, however, as he peered across the room at the ornately outfitted operating table, next to which stood Victor… and the real Henry Jekyll.

Christmas Eve responded to her fairy friends' wailing with lightning reflexes. Soaring majestically down from the gabled rooftop on which she had been perched, Eve quickly grabbed the frightening bull mastiff by the scruff of the neck, his enormous canines mere inches from Noel's backside. Hoisting the maddened, slobbering dog upward so that his eyes were level with hers, Eve began shaking the hound and waggling her finger at him.

"Bad doggie!" scolded Eve.

The surprised hound recoiled slightly, staring daggers at the Yuletide heroine. He started to lunge at her, but Eve forcefully yanked him away by the nape of the neck again and reiterated her displeasure.

"Ut!" she admonished, staring down the beast until he averted his eyes in submission.

The great animal started to curl up the left side of his jowls in a halfhearted snarl, but Eve defeated that gesture by placing her waggling index finger aside of his snout and barking out a command.

"Sit! Stay!" she growled.

Setting the dog down on the ground, Eve tenderly released her hold on the great beast. The dog whimpered slightly, lowering his mammoth head down between his immense front paws. As if genuflecting, the bull mastiff raised his hind end high into the air and started to imploringly wag his tail, waiting sheepishly for Eve's next command.

"Who's my good doggie?" Eve effused in a lilting sing-song voice.

The great hound was elated. He began prancing around Eve and the girls, emitting playful barks and licking them all. The Sugar Plum Fairies giggled lightheartedly at their former foe's antics, even though his rough, slobbery tongue was bigger than any of their three heads. Everything was just settling down when they heard the clacking of running feet echoing along the fog slick cobblestones. Christmas Eve stood stoically to face whatever dangers this new disturbance might bring, while the great hound cowered behind her, with the girls peeking out from behind him.

"The bloody hound went this way, Holmes!" came a deep, baritone voice from out of the fog, followed closely by a portly, mustachioed middle aged man, well dressed and brandishing a pearl handled British Army issue revolver.

"Lead on, my dear Watson!" came the reply in a sharp, crisp commanding voice with just the slightest hint of a nasal twang, "The beast must be collared! There's danger about and the game's afoot!"

As the two men rounded the corner, Eve began smiling at the stark contrast between them. For all of the portly man's slouch and bluster, his companion maintained a lanky whippet-like posture, clean shaven with sharp features and a pointed needle-like nose. He wore a tweed overcoat and stole with a matching deerstalker hat. His steely, deep set eyes darted about, observing every aspect of his surroundings and his commanding demeanor let all gathered know that he was the man in charge.

"Don't you dare lay a hand on this dog!" warned Eve, quickly grasping the first fellow's revolver and disarming him completely.

"I say, Miss," sputtered the portly man known as Watson, "You're interfering with a murder investigation being conducted by the great Sherlock Holmes! This hound is suspected of killing one Lord Baskerville and several members of his family!"

Watson was about to lay further into Eve when his gaze shot past her and settled on Holly, Noel and Carol. He recoiled in abject terror.

"Bloody Hell, Holmes! Imps! Demons! Goblins in taffeta!" bellowed Watson, "I warned you this case contained elements of the supernatural and how right I was!"

"We're not 'taffy head goblins'," whined Carol, "We're Sugar Plum Fairies!"

"Yeah! Watch who you're calling an 'imp', bub!" griped Noel.

"Are you REALLY Sherlock Holmes?" asked Holly in wonderment and awe.

"Indeed I am, young miss," offered Holmes, doffing his hat to the ladies, "At your service."

"You're rather accepting of all this rot and balderdash, Holmes," remarked Watson rather snidely, "Whatever happened to your well-known Holmsian skepticism?"

"As I always admonish you, my dear Dr. Watson, when you've ruled out the impossible, whatever remains, however improbable, must be the truth," quipped Holmes, "I believe a conference with these fine young ladies and their statuesque chaperone would serve us all well."

Well, then…" began Christmas Eve, "Let me tell you about a Yeti named Charlie…"

Henry Cobbler sat amid the reeds and tall grass of the swale near the old haunted grist mill, dangling his bare feet in the cool, clear water, with only one thought on his mind -- his proximity to Guinevere Upington-Smythe. This girl, this confounding, annoying, wonderful creature was all Henry Cobbler could think about. There was no real reason he should be so drawn to her. They were polar opposites. But, Henry, nonetheless, could scarce contain his excitement over Guinevere's lithe form sitting so close to his, hidden from the world in the thicket of bull rushes.

Henry found his throat growing increasingly drier and his heartbeat so loud it nearly drowned out the incessant chirping and buzzing of the nearby crickets and dragonflies. Summoning every ounce of intestinal fortitude his scant fifteen years of life afforded him, Henry cleared his crackling dry throat and attempted his heretofore greatest feat of druidic magic -- small talk.

"Good old Ferret," he croaked, "he gets right down to the business at hand, doesn't he?"

The two teens watched their third companion, Ferret Reynolds, crawl, meander in a serpentine crouch, roll, slither and generally stagger across the meadow on the opposite side of the brook in a somewhat comical effort to evade, well, nothing in particular, all the while encumbered by a hefty length of bull rope that he hoped to use in setting a snare for the rumored Yeti, recently sighted on the grounds of Stonehenge Academy.

"So it would seem," remarked Guinevere distantly, casually gazing at Ferret while tickling Henry's ear with a tall blade of meadow grass.

"He's been my best mate for some time now, but I like you, as well, Gwen," Henry stammered, hoping his words wouldn't be met with too much rejection or derision. Sensing none, Henry pressed his advantage.

"We ARE friends, aren't we, Gwen?" Henry questioned.

A ruckus arose across the pond as Ferret, attempting to stealthily shinny up a birch tree, got his rope snagged on a root and was unceremoniously yanked to the ground amidst a flurry of dry leaves, dust clouds and obscenities. Dusting himself off, he gave Henry and Guinevere a thumb's up, untangled the rope and wound it around his shoulder and headed up the tree again. Guinevere stifled a giggle and turned her attention back to Henry.

Drawing closer to Henry, so close that their cheeks were mere centimeters apart and her breath fogged up his spectacles, Guinevere whispered in Henry's ear.

"Of course we're friends, Henry Cobbler. Good friends. Friends that can say anything to one another," she whispered coyly.

Henry's heart almost leaped out of his chest and did an end zone victory dance across the pasture! Guinevere, sweet, sweet Guinevere, his star-crossed soul mate, the girl of his dreams, was about to profess her reciprocal feelings! Perhaps she sensed his shyness and, as all life companions are wont to do, felt his reluctance to speak the words aloud and empathically decided to do it for him! In any case, Henry's mind wildly swirled with thoughts of bridal registry china patterns and both boy and girl baby names.

"Of course, dear," Henry effused, "we CAN say anything to one another! Anything at all! Even the words 'I love…'"

"Then, tell me, Henry," interjected Guinevere, excitedly bolting upright, striking to the heart of the matter, "is Ferret seeing anyone? He's quite a striking specimen of young manhood, wot?"

"I love… good old Ferret like a brother," continued Henry, growing flushed with embarrassment, "and he'd make a fine catch for any young girl and, no, he isn't spoken for. Yes. Good. Old. Ferret. Ha Ha."

Peering across the glade at his gangly chum awkwardly trying to shinny up the birch while Guinevere sighed dreamily in Ferret's direction, no longer knowing or caring if Henry were there in the swale with her or not, Henry couldn't help but postulate the odds of his dear, dear pal slipping from a branch and accidentally hanging himself by his own bull rope.

As the two scientists and the floating bundle of clothing that was The Invisible Man approached him menacingly, Charlie began to get the feeling that victuals and drink were not at all in his immediate future. He backed warily towards the laboratory door, waving massive paws at his assailants and growling defensively.

"Who are you, sir, and why did you impersonate Edward Hyde?" quizzed The Invisible Man.

"I never said I was Hyde," snarled Charlie, "You just assumed that!"

"And you did nothing to dissuade me of that notion," spat The Invisible Man.

"I can't believe that you thought this hairy, unkempt chap was my alter ego," mused Henry Jekyll, "How little regard you have for your friends!"

"Can you blame him?" chided Victor Von Frankenstein, "Your other self, Edward, is hardly a shining example of gentility. Quite the contrary as I'm told by my colleagues back in London."

"You have colleagues?" japed Jekyll, "Will the wonders of The Fade never cease?"

"Why, you bloated, uncouth lout," started Victor.

Charlie The Yeti stood slightly bemused by the three supposed gentlemen's bickering, but not for long. Slowly backing up, he glanced about the room for a weapon to use against the trio of aggressors. Charlie found none.

"Never a club or a board with a rusty nail sticking out around when you really need one," groused Charlie under his breath.

Charlie continued his wary backward steps until he felt the door frame poke into the small of his back. Cautiously playing his massive hand over the surface of the rough wooden door, Charlie feigned nonchalance, continuing his litany of lies to his suddenly hostile hosts, until his paw gripped the latch. Henry, Victor and The Invisible Man drew ever closer, brandishing a scalpel, bone saw and a jagged edged broken glass beaker respectively, all the while sizing up their quarry and looking for an opening to strike. Charlie, having sneakily and silently unfastened the latch behind his back, slowly turned it until the door grew slightly ajar. This was Charlie's chance! All he needed now was a sly, momentary diversion to deflect his enemies' gazes.

"Eek! A bat!" bellowed Charlie, pointing above and behind his assailants.

"Where? Where?" they chimed in unison, turning to look.

Whirling on his massive feet, Charlie bolted through the door into the hallway and began scampering down the long corridor towards freedom. The scientists and their see-through compatriot gave chase, but were summarily stymied by the inadvertent appearance of Victor's hunchbacked servant, whom Charlie easily hoisted over his head and hurled at the hapless trio, scattering them like ten pins across the cobblestones of the hallway. As they regained their feet, Victor, Henry and The Invisible Man were just in time to see Charlie hurl himself out a stained glass window onto the patio, across the courtyard and over the stone wall surrounding the castle keep.

"Shall we give chase, Victor?" queried Henry Jekyll.

"No need," sighed Victor. "I've been having neighbor problems with the villagers of late. They've mustered quite the neighborhood watch against me and it shan't be long before they give our mal-odorous intruder chase."

True to his assertion, Victor's neighbors, having had their fill of the strange goings on at the castle, took none too kindly to the massive, hairy form that leapt into their midst, screaming like a banshee on fire. Rousing from slumber, the villagers hastily lit torches, grabbed farming implements and took off in hot pursuit of Charlie. Menacingly brandishing their pick axes, shovels, rakes and pitchforks, the ragtag mob chased Charlie clear past the outskirts of town and only stopped when the Yeti crossed over into another region of The Fade, watching as Charlie yowled and darted past the horizon. No, Charlie The Yeti had never before been chased by villagers with torches and pitchforks and he did not like it one little bit, especially sans food, drink and a ride.

END CHAPTER SEVEN

Chapter Eight

Christmas Eve and the Sugar Plum Fairies, having concluded their story, were thoroughly enjoying their stroll through fog-enshrouded Victorian London. Sherlock Holmes, despite his stern demeanor and piercing, searching eyes, was quite the raconteur. Doctor Watson, too, was quick with a jovial riposte and had a vigorous, infectious laugh. Carol, in particular, loved his anecdotes and took to calling him "Unca John", much to the bemusement of Holmes.

"So, my fine ladies," began Holmes effusively, "If I may summarize your current situation, you are in dogged pursuit of this boorish Charlie The Yeti chap in an effort to reclaim the lost Golden Garland of Zeus for Father Christmas before such time as he's forced to cancel his annual yuletide journey.

"Further," he continued, brow furrowed in deep concentration, "Your map and Hera's ring have led you here, where we've all become fast friends, despite your very existence causing Watson and I to rethink everything we have known to be real, heretofore. Does that about cover it?"

"Quite, Holmes, old chap," blustered Dr. John Watson, "But, you've yet to answer Miss Holly's question of why this Charlie bounder would pilfer something up north, travel to Tibet, only to meander his way back north where he began?"

"Did you say all that, Holly?" mewled Carol, "I didn't know your mouth was big enough to say all those words!"

"HA! 'Bounder'," smirked Noel, "Good one, Hol'..!"

"I never, but I didn't…" sputtered Holly.

"Girls! Settle!" snapped Christmas Eve.

"Quite all right, my dear," reassured Holmes, "Your girls MUST be silly. They can't help themselves. It's their natures. In fact, that is the supposition I'm employing in formulating my conclusion in regards to Charlie's strange, circuitous route. There is NO logic to his actions, therefore, I must assume he has done so for reasons of instinct or, perhaps, family matters, whose particulars we are not privy to. "

"Family matters? Really, Holmes," scoffed Watson.

"My dear doctor, have you ever known any family to act logically where one of their own is concerned?" retorted Holmes.

"Quite!" acquiesced Watson.

"Lacking those all-important puzzle pieces, I cannot give a more concrete answer." said Holmes sadly, noticeably vexed by a problem he couldn't solve.

"That's okay, Mr. Holmes," conciliated Carol, "I like your hat, anyway."

Smiling warmly for a moment at Carol's innocence, Holmes collected himself and began to instruct Eve on the best way to proceed.

"We'd like to help you, Miss Eve," Holmes said, "But we have somewhat of a sticky wicket ourselves to handle with this Baskerville business. I can, however, point you in the right direction to continue your quest. See that castle yonder along the horizon? Go there. Perhaps the denizens of that fabled realm may be of further assistance to you. They do seem predisposed to quests and all sorts of magical folderol. Go hence, and good hunting to you all!"

"Thank you, sir," replied Christmas Eve, "But, what is that place? It looks far more medieval than where we are now."

"I believe," interjected Dr. Watson, "The citizens thereabouts call it 'Camelot'."

Ferret Reynolds was struggling to unhook his ankle from a tight crook between tree branches on the imposing birch, flopping upside down like a huge, convulsive marlin that had just been reeled in by a portly, middle-aged fisherman on holiday. Although the blood rushing to his head caused his freckles to merge into one huge russet blob, making Ferret look quite ridiculous in Henry Cobbler's estimation, Guinevere Upington-Smythe sighed and cooed with admiration. Just as Henry Cobbler was smitten with Guinevere, so, too, was she enamored of Ferret Reynolds.

Henry Cobbler's eyes began to sting as he endeavored to hold back his tears. For most of his life, Henry was alone in the world but now, cruel fate had decreed that his best friend, possibly his ONLY friend, should catch the fancy of the one girl in all the universe Henry considered to be his "soul mate". Love's infernal triangle had struck again!

"I think Ferret needs help," whispered Guinevere, still mostly hidden in the rushes with Henry.

"Nah," growled Henry, "Ferret does this sort of thing quite often."

"Really?" asked Guinevere incredulously.

"Oh, yes. He's always on about some uncoordinated bit of

mischief," oiled Henry rather jealously, "A bit of a fop, really."

"Nonetheless, Henry, I think we should go to him. He's turning blue," squealed Guinevere.

Leaving their place of concealment amidst the reeds and tall grass of the brook which ran alongside of the old, haunted grist mill, Henry couldn't help but notice the concern etched on Guinevere's face for their friend. He wondered if he were in similar straits, perhaps with his arm caught in a badger trap or lungs ready to collapse from a bout of Cholera, would Gwen be quite as upset for his well-being? His self-pitying musings were interrupted, however, by loud bellowing from off in the distance, beyond the grist mill, just past a line of fir trees, in the middle of a briar patch. The roar gave a broad indication of a beast of some size… a beast that was heading in their direction! Ferret began waving his arms frantically at his companions.

"Cor, then, ye two! Bit of an 'and here, wot?!" exclaimed Ferret. "My trap is nigh well sprung!"

"On yourself, it appears," remarked Henry, with just a touch of sarcasm in his voice.

"Henry Cobbler! You get over here and help me free Ferret!" chided Guinevere Upington-Smythe.

Henry wasn't sure which stung more, Gwen's chiding of him or the underlying concern for Ferret mixed in with her words. In any event, Henry supposed that Ferret was a right enough chap not to be left as monster bait regardless of Gwen's misguided feelings for him. Henry began to hoist Ferret up so that he could unhook his wedged foot but, no sooner did Ferret extricate his foot than he began flailing at Henry.

"The rope, 'Enry Cobbler! Give us the rope and don't lollygag! We've a Yeti to capture!" sputtered Ferret, the natural color just starting to return to his ruddy face.

"But, I was just trying to…" stammered Henry in self-defense.

"Lord love a duck! Give me the bloody rope!" rebuked Ferret.

"Really, Henry!" scolded Guinevere, "If you're not going to help, you shouldn't have come on this expedition in the first place!"

While Ferret struggled to tie a proper slip knot in the cumbersome rope, with Guinevere looking on approvingly and encouraging Ferret's actions, the loud roaring grew closer. Henry sat quietly on a nearby stump, fiddling with a long blade of grass between his fingers and hoping for all the world that, rather than a Yeti, it might actually be a hungry Tyrannosaurus Rex come to devour them all.

Charlie The Yeti had been running for what seemed like hours. It had been, in fact, no more than ten minutes. Either way, the overweight and out of shape beast was spent. He wasn't quite sure where he was, having dropped his map in the melee with the Transylvanian villagers, but Charlie was almost certain that he was in quite a different realm of The Fade than he had previously been.

As he sat down beneath a rock outcropping, Charlie dipped his aching feet into a pool of cool mountain water formed by a rivulet issuing forth from a cleft in the surrounding rocks. While the frigid waters soothed his throbbing bunions, Charlie took stock of his travails thus far.

"I've been chased by villagers with pitchforks, accosted by evil scientists and invisible madmen and held at sword point by French Musketeers and I'm getting just a little fed up with the whole thing," snarled Charlie to no one in particular.

"What good is this stupid garland swag if I can't use it to go from one end of The Fade to another without all this hassle?" Charlie asked himself "I just want to visit my Uncle Grimfang! All I'm looking for is a free ride, some free food and drink and for people to leave me alone! Is that too much to ask? Whatever happened to all that vaunted Christmas charity everyone keeps yammering about? Huh? I ask you…"

Charlie's bitter reverie was suddenly interrupted by the sound of voices just over the rise behind him. Fearing the mountain villagers had maybe called ahead to their friends in the next territory, Charlie stealthily crept up the rocky embankment and furtively peeked over the rock outcropping. If he was being hunted down by Texas Rangers from the Russian Steppes or Canadian Mounties in Constantinople or something equally ridiculous as that, he was going to turn the tables and get the jump on them first.

What Charlie saw, however, was not some erstwhile posse anxious to cash in on an APB but, rather, a caravan of camels hauling all sorts of exotic wares across a desert trade route. Finely woven Persian rugs, rare jewels, furs from unusual animals far and wide and exquisitely hand carved bottles of sweet smelling perfumes were all in evidence. Charlie had no use for such things as those and was about to return to his foot bath when he caught whiff of a camel laden with succulent food stuffs.

"Food and a ride," mused Charlie, "This seems to be my day, after all! Perhaps I can follow along at a safe distance and when they stop for the night, I can make off with my booty."

Congratulating himself on his own cleverness with a nod and a sly chuckle, Charlie began to lope along behind the caravan, out of sight, just beyond the crest of the hill. They hadn't gone more than a mile, though, when the camels were startled by loud whoops and hollers, echoing across the desert. Turning quickly to his right, Charlie saw hordes of riders on horseback, galloping over the sand dunes, brandishing scimitars and driving full bore towards the helpless caravan.

"Of course…" growled Charlie as he sat down on the hillside with his head in his hands, sobbing through gritted teeth.

Fifteen minutes after the attack, when the caravan drivers had been routed and the camels and merchandise plundered, the robber hordes took off over the dunes in an easterly direction, their camel laden swag in tow. They were moving much slower now due to their added burden and Charlie decided to continue with his original plan and follow from a safe distance.

"Stealing a camel and some food from a merchant or a bandit… it's all the same to me," determined Charlie as he continued to wend his way across the dunes at a safe distance, after first stopping to check the slain merchants for anything of potential value to him like, say, a wineskin or canteen.

Finding nothing, Charlie continued on his way, thinking to himself that he'd been in The Fade long enough to know that, within a few hours, these men would all be revived back at the start of their caravan trade route, ready to begin the whole tableau all over again. That's the nature of The Fade. Its residents could not be harmed for long, only outsiders such as himself or Santa Claus were ever in any real danger. That's why Charlie was glad he had the Golden Garland and why he knew Santa would never risk coming after him without it.

Charlie, of course, had no idea that Christmas Eve and the Sugar Plum Fairies were pursuing him, nor would he care over much if he had known. Charlie was only ever concerned with what was good for Charlie at any given moment.

It was just after dusk when Charlie The Yeti stole up to the bandit encampment. Though improbably large, even for a Yeti, Charlie held stealth as his credo. He had pulled off the crime of the century by stealing the Golden Garland right out from under Santa's nose. Surely, he thought, pilfering a leg of mutton and one smallish camel would pose no difficulty for him. Charlie The Yeti never ran dry of his reservoir for being wrong.

His raid on the larder was successful enough but Charlie had no sooner grabbed the reins of one of the camels, a large mutton shank tucked beneath his arm, when the skittish beast of burden let out an ear piercing screech that echoed throughout the camp. Within seconds, Charlie was surrounded by scimitar wielding brigands. Armed only with the hindquarter of meat, Charlie was, nonetheless, determined to make their victory a costly one, swinging it wildly about his head like a Louisville Slugger, hoping to connect with the skull of any bandit who got too close.

"C'mon, ya hoodlums," barked Charlie, "Let ol' Charlie school ya in how we do things back in the frozen north!"

The bandits stood at a safe distance, puzzled. Most of them had never seen a Yeti before. As they were sizing him up, one of them caught a glimpse of the Golden Garland hanging out of the top of Charlie's lederhosen.

"AIEEE! This furry white one has the Golden Garland of Zeus in his possession! Alert the chieftain!" the astonished brigand exclaimed.

A barely audible buzz murmured through the camp and soon the sea of bandits parted and bowed to an authoritative figure who strode through their ranks straight towards Charlie.

"That's right! I have the garland," spat Charlie, "And that gives me free passage through your domain. I don't want no trouble with you Hottentots, so just back off an' me and my mutton and that camel over yonder will be on our way! Savvy?"

The tribal chieftain, dressed in furs and leather, with iron studded wrist bands, a jewel handled sword and a horned helmet, stood and stared coolly at the agitated Yeti. He didn't twitch. He didn't flinch, even when one of Charlie's wild swings came dangerously close to his head. After a few moments, Charlie got it into his head that the bandit leader was not intimidated and would not back down. Charlie settled down and warily lowered the deadly sheep shank, not taking his eyes off any of them for even one second.

"You're a cool one, I'll give you that," remarked Charlie with just the slightest tinge of admiration in his feral voice, "Okay, it's your play… what's the skinny, Jimmy?"

The chieftain drummed his hand casually atop his sword's gem encrusted pommel and his eyes were flinty slits. After several tense moments of a standoff between the intractable bandit leader and the mutton wielding mountain Yeti, the face-off ended when the robber baron broke into a wide grin.

"These are my warrior Huns," the chieftain said calmly, "My name is Attila. We should talk."

END CHAPTER EIGHT

Chapter Nine

Christmas Eve and the girls had left Victorian London far behind them and were about halfway up the rolling hillside leading to Camelot when they stopped for lunch beside a placid lake set back amidst a leafy glade.

"There aren't any swans here, Eve," remarked Holly, "So we should be able to eat in peace."

"I hope there aren't any 'amacongas', either," blurted Carol.

"Dibs on the bologna!" shouted Noel.

Following a quick lunch, while Eve was replacing the dishes and utensils back into the magical pocket inside her cloak's lining, Holly, Noel and Carol passed the time with an impromptu stone skipping contest across the tranquil forest lake.

"Five… six… seven… eight…" counted Holly, "I'm winning!"

"No way!" yelled Noel, "That was only seven! That last one was a plunk, not a skip!"

"Was too!" countered Holly.

"Not!" argued Noel

"My turn! My turn!" wheedled Carol.

The other two Sugar Plums stopped bickering long enough to watch their sister take her turn. Carol, one eye shut, tongue protruding out of the side of her mouth, wound up and let fly with her perfectly flat stony projectile. Skip, skip, skip, KER-TANG! Her stone's trajectory was suddenly and rudely interrupted by the shaft of a gleaming sword rising from the froth, being upheld by an alabaster woman's hand.

"Huh. That's different," remarked Holly with mild surprise.

"I win! I win!" shouted Noel.

"No fair! No fair! Interference!" wailed Carol.

The girls' caterwauling alerted Eve and the First Lady of Yuletide Cheer hurtled towards the lake unmindful of any potential danger, seeking only to protect her tiny friends. As she neared the shore, Eve could see the fairies leaping and flitting about, pointing to the disturbance in the center of the lake.

"Eve! There's a lady out there with a sword!" cried Holly.

"She might be drowneded-ing!" moaned Carol.

"Maybe she's sword fishing," snarked Noel.

Eve surveyed the scene and, sure enough, the girls were correct. There, in the center of the otherwise placid body of water, was, indeed, a slender woman's arm holding a magnificent golden sword that glistened and gleamed in the midday sunlight. Christmas Eve, under normal circumstances, would have paid scant heed to the odd tableau but, here in The Fade, without the benefit of the Golden Garland of Zeus to provide them safe harbor, she was unwilling to take chances with possible peril. Arcing high into the noonday sun, Christmas Eve gracefully executed a perfect jack-knife dive, swooped low over the surface of the water and wrested the shining weapon from the grasp of its female handler. Barrel rolling and somersaulting through the air, Eve lightly landed on the near bank with her prize as her Sugar Plum Fairy comrades excitedly gathered around her.

"That was AWESOME," admired Holly, "You were better even than Michael Phelps!"

"Aw, I coulda done that, I betcha," added Noel.

"C'n I see the sword, Christmas Eve?" asked Carol, "It's pretty!"

The other two fairies took their cue from Carol and quickly began pestering Eve to see, touch and play with the deadly sharp weapon. Eve, for her part, realized that, though the girls were possibly centuries old, they were much more like children than anything else and letting children play around with sharp objects would land you on Santa's Naughty List for sure!

Looking around for a scabbard to sheathe the shimmering blade in, however, generated no results for the harried Christmas super heroine. Eve then began to intently scour the surrounding terrain for a makeshift housing for the weapon and, off in the distance, she spied a rather large boulder resting in the middle of the plain several hundred yards shy of the castle walls. Leaping gracefully skyward, Christmas Eve dropped down directly in front of the boulder and, utilizing strength as great as Santa's love for the children, thrust the golden sword hilt deep into the imposing granite stone.

"That should keep the sword out of careless, prying Fairy hands," smirked Eve, "Or anyone else's, for that matter."

The three fairy sisters fluttered up to Christmas Eve, alternately excited and impressed by her heroic prowess and disappointed that they wouldn't be able to play with the pretty, shiny, deadly sword.

"Wow! Nobody's EVER gonna be able to pull that ol' sword outta that rock," crowed Holly.

"Aw, I bet if you wiggled it enough, you could get it loose enough to slip out," replied Noel, trying to downplay her admiration for Eve's feat of strength.

"Oh, that poor rock!" blubbered Carol, "I hope you didn't hurt him too bad, Eve!"

With that, the girls started loudly arguing whether stones were even alive, let alone could feel anything. Eve, flustered at her friends' seeming obliviousness to the ever-present danger facing them at every turn in The Fade without the Golden Garland, tried to hush their yammering, to no avail. Suddenly, a voice that sounded like leaves crackling on a roaring bonfire interrupted the mayhem.

"And so, The Prophesy is fulfilled! The events of destiny set into motion! You, M' lady, have this day reaped the undying appreciation of the all-powerful magician, Merlin!"

Charlie The Yeti was supremely cunning but not particularly bright. As he rode alongside Attila The Hun at the head of the column of Hun bandits, belly full, astride a fiery stallion, Charlie was perplexed. His furrowed, bushy brow betrayed his consternation to the warrior chieftain and Attila addressed him warmly.

"What seems to be the problem, Charlie my friend?" roared Attila jovially, "Not thinking of reneging on our agreement, are you?"

"Why no, Attila, my boon companion," lied the wily beast man, "We both are getting exactly what we want without unnecessary bloodshed."

Charlie, in fact, was trying to think of a way to extricate himself from his current situation. It seemed like a good idea at the time, when surrounded by a hoard of Hunnish mountain bandits, to negotiate his current pact with Attila. It didn't take much cajoling on Charlie's part to offer a trade of possession of the Golden Garland of Zeus in exchange for food, beverage and a ride to Tibet to visit his uncle. Charlie explained to the anxious Hun leader that with the Garland in his possession, Attila was free to ride roughshod over ALL the realms of The Fade, cutting a swath of banditry such as this world had never seen. He further sweetened the pot by "explaining" that the Garland was only effective if given freely as a gift and should Attila simply try to take it from him, not only would Charlie heft a mean mutton shank, resulting in many bruised and broken Huns, it would be rendered useless to anyone. But, Charlie clarified, his asking price was slight when compared to the riches the Huns would reap with the Garland in their employ.

Attila The Hun thought for several minutes of all the booty he and his savage hordes could command in exchange for some trifles that were stolen anyway and a bargain was struck. But now, Charlie was having second thoughts. Of course, everything he'd told Attila was a bald faced lie and the Hun chieftain could just take the Garland from Charlie, but the Yeti was far more worried about how he'd get back to the North Pole after he surrendered the Garland. Plus, he mused, if Attila was so willing to form a pact, there was probably far more advantage for Charlie in holding on to the Garland.

"Curse my inability to see the big picture," groused Charlie under his breath, "It must be a genetic trait. Now, I'm stuck with this boorish lout until I can think of some way to dissolve our contract without serious harm to myself."

Charlie's ruminations were abruptly interrupted when the Hunnish hordes began a loud, lusty cheer. The Tibetan settlement of Charlie's Uncle Grimfang was in sight.

Henry Cobbler had a name for his misery. It was Ferret Reynolds. From his seat on the stump near the birch tree that Ferret was trying to erect a Yeti trap on, with only a bull rope and the approving, doe-eyed ogling of Guinevere Upington-Smythe, Henry

wondered what he had ever seen in Mister Ferret Reynolds that allowed him to let his guard down long enough to call the freckled fop
"friend".

"That rope's far too heavy to allow the branch to snap back in the
manner you propose," offered the young, bespectacled druid in
training.

"Is it now, 'Mister Yeti Trap Expert', 'Enry Cobbler?" snarked
Ferret Reynolds, trying to free several fingers he'd inadvertently
gotten interwoven with his "special" slip knot, "I suppose you can
do better then, hey?"

"No," replied Henry, "There are no heavier branches hereabouts
and no time to dig a proper tiger pit. The thrashing and growling
seem to be getting closer far too rapidly for that."

"Really, Henry!" snapped Guinevere Upington-Smythe, "Why
didn't you offer these helpful suggestions before poor Ferret started
implementing your ill-conceived plan? If you have nothing constructive to add, perhaps you'd best just run along back to the dorms,
then, wot?"

"But I never…" started Henry.

"Blimey, Bird! 'oo put the bee in your bonnet, eh?" shot back
Ferret, "'Enry's me best mate an' don't think sendin' 'im away's
gonna get you any piece of the reward f'r capturing the bloody Yeti!
Females is a jinx on safari or Bob's y'r uncle, says I!"

Things fell apart rapidly for the trio, then. Ferret and Guinevere
started quarreling like an old married couple and Henry, trying to
break up the duo, got shoved backwards and tripped over the
stump, losing his glasses in the fall. As he was groping along the
ground for his spectacles, Henry heard a feral roar, followed by a
piercing scream from Guinevere, followed by an equally high-
pitched squeal from Ferret. Looking up from behind his stump,
Henry, though his vision was rather blurry at that point, saw what
appeared to his myopic eyesight to be the biggest bear he'd ever

seen chase his two friends across the meadow and into a thick grove of willow trees.

"Hmm," Henry thought to himself, calmly putting his glasses back on after wiping them off on the sleeve of his Stonehenge Academy blazer, "That must've been the Yeti that Custodian Homberg offered the reward for. I hope he doesn't maim my friends too badly when he catches them. That would be a downright shame."

Charlie The Yeti clung tightly to the undercarriage of The Orient Express as it pulled into Calais on the French coast. His fingers were numb from the cold and he couldn't feel the metal rods that connected the axle to the coach above, but he had lashed himself to the train with the Golden Garland of Zeus in such a way that he couldn't fall off even if he fell asleep and lost his grip, which he had done several times during the long journey from Constantinople to the English Channel.

"It won't be long until we cross the channel to London," Charlie reassured himself, "Then I can finally stretch my legs and get out of this cursed wind."

As the Conductor gave last call and the train lurched out of the station, bound for London, Charlie thought back on all the trouble he had getting to this point beginning with his ill-fated trip to Tibet.

"There's a portion of my life I'll never get back," Charlie spat as he pondered his decision to visit his Uncle Grimfang.

"Whatever possessed me to think that visiting relatives around the holidays would be a good thing?" he wondered aloud, his voice trailing off into the wind.

It seemed like weeks to Charlie, but who could really tell inside The Fade? Time had no real meaning here. In any event, there was Charlie, leading a column of marauding Huns up to the very doorstep of the mountain village of the Tibetan Yetis and Charlie's own uncle. Charlie, still deep in thought pondering a way out of his bargain with Attila to turn over the Golden Garland to the Hun chieftain as soon as Charlie was safely delivered to his Uncle Grimfang, didn't notice the growing agitation on the faces of the bandit hordes as they made their way through the narrow mountain pass.

Sheer cliff faces lined either side of the tight trail, which narrowed to the point that the Huns could only ride single file. Their furtive glances upward, scanning each tor for signs of movement indicated that they were all aware that this would be the perfect place for an ambush. They weren't wrong. No sooner had the last Hunnish rider entered the gorge than a thunderous rumbling began and a rockslide of epic proportions cascaded down and filled in the trail head, blocking their rear flank and any hopes of escape, with a contingent of Yetis capering and gibbering with glee atop the crag at a job well done.

"We are besieged!" bellowed Attila, sword upraised, horse rearing up on hind legs, "Forward to the village! Leave no one left standing! Today, we plunder!"

"Now, wait a minute…" started Charlie, but he was soon drowned out by the flinty clip clop of galloping horses' hooves over the granite stones as the furious riders urged their steeds past the hesitant Yeti, jostling him to one side and pinning him against one of the cliff walls. It was all a bitter misunderstanding. The Tibetan Yetis were only trying to protect their homes from the fabled Attila The Hun who, in his turn, was living up to his fearsome reputation to take any opportunity to pillage the innocent, and the rockslide was more than enough reason.

"This is NOT good!" yelped Charlie, face firmly planted against the solid granite wall of the mountain pass.

When the column had finally squeezed past him and he could move his horse towards the village again, Charlie was overwhelmed by the cacophonous sounds of battle coming from the Yeti hamlet. Spurring his skittish horse forward, Charlie galloped into town, hoping to size up the situation and, at the very least, rescue his uncle from harm. As he entered the town square, however, Charlie was confronted by a slew of Yeti berserkers, brandishing stone axes, clubs and fair sized boulders. They were caught up in the bloodlust of the battle and it made no difference to them that Charlie, apparently, was one of them. They were about the business of protecting their homes from the invading Huns and attacked anyone or anything on horseback.

Ducking beneath their blows and fending off rocks with his upraised forearm (and sometimes his head), Charlie careened his mount around a corner and quickly dismounted, hoping to blend in with the Yeti warriors. This action proved to be not much better as plans go. Once off his horse, Charlie was nigh well indistinguishable from the Tibetan Yetis and became fair game for the slashing blades and thundering hooves of the mounted Hunnish brigands.

"I can't win for losing," Charlie shouted, as he dove to his left, narrowly avoiding a beheading from the flashing scimitar of a marauding Hun rider.

As he hit the ground, Charlie tucked and rolled out of the way and began scrabbling for cover in a serpentine crawl, skinning his elbows and knees in the process. When he finally reached the relative safety of an overturned hay wagon, Charlie burrowed beneath the hay for camouflage and tried to catch his breath and reclaim his wits. When his breathing slowed and the roaring in his ears lessened somewhat, Charlie heard a sound coming from behind a nearby watering trough. It was the sound of breathing. Someone else was hiding close by. Screwing up his courage, Charlie crouched on his haunches, waited until a column of three Huns galloped past and made a daring leap towards the trough, missing the mark by several feet and scrambling on hands and knees for cover. When he finally plopped down in a ragged heap behind the trough and the spots before his eyes eased enough for his vision to clear, Charlie caught his first glimpse of his fellow skulker. The family resemblance was unmistakable. It was Charlie's Uncle Grimfang.

"Hello, nephew," snarled Grimfang sardonically.

Chapter Ten

Henry Cobbler strolled nonchalantly towards the hilltop just beyond the old, haunted grist mill, enjoying the dappled sunlight peeking through the branches of the willow trees. He knew he should be about the business of rescuing his friends, Ferret Reynolds and Guinevere Upington-Smythe, but the resplendent beauty of the day was just too joyous to waste.

"A shame about my mates being chased by a yeti… or bear… I'm not sure which, exactly," grinned Henry as he paused to listen to a robin's song.

In the past several hours, Henry Cobbler had been dragged from the comfortable confines of his dorm room at the Stonehenge Academy, cajoled into taking part in an ill-conceived, poorly planned yeti safari, had his heart broken by the girl of his dreams, been verbally humiliated for offering constructive suggestions on snare building and been rudely shoved to the ground by his supposed friends while trying to break up an argument between the two of them. It was little wonder, then, that Henry was in no real hurry to fly to his friends' aid. Oh, he'd endeavor to rescue them eventually. Henry wasn't that petty. But a little hesitation probably couldn't hurt Ferret and Guinevere overmuch.

"They're quick," he thought to himself, "Plus, the beast isn't likely to eat them both right away even if he does catch them."

And, too, Henry mused, it would be quite soothing to his ruffled ego to be able to say "I told you so" to Ferret in regards to the latter's trap building prowess after a dramatic last minute rescue.

"How splendid," crowed Henry, "A spider weaving his web! This deserves a bit of a watch, now, doesn't it?"

After about ten minutes of web gazing, Henry sighed, stood up, brushed off the seat of his knickers and ambled up the hill again.

"Time to save the day, I suppose," heaved Henry stoically.

Christmas Eve and the Sugar Plum Fairies stood in the shadow of the castle keep and stared blankly at Merlin the Magician. After proper introductions had been made, the sorcerer, stoop shouldered with age and leaning on a gnarled wooden staff, smiled at the foursome from beneath thick grey whiskers and cracked, dry wrinkles that seemed to encompass his entire face. From within the folds of his dingy, ill-fitting russet tunic, covered with inelegantly sewn on crescent moon and stars iconography, Merlin poked out a withered, palsied hand, pointed at the girls, cleared his throat and began to speak.

"Today, M' lady, thee hast furthered the cause of justice and set in motion the wheels of glorious destiny with thy simple action."

"I was only trying to protect my friends from hurting themselves on that dangerously sharp sword," explained Christmas Eve.

"We can't help it. We like shiny things," offered Holly.

"And swords are so cool," added Noel.

"We're pretty silly sometimes," interjected Carol, looking up from playing with a caterpillar, "It's what we do."

"Thy motives notwithstanding, my children, and that you acted out of love and concern only sweetens the outcome of thine actions, look ye yonder at what thou hast wrought," chuckled Merlin, pointing to the rock that Eve had thrust the sword into.

Gathered around the large boulder were numerous knights and their squires. They had all queued up and were taking turns trying to extricate the weapon from its granite sheath in an impromptu contest of strength. Though many of them were imposingly large and strong of sinew, try as they may, none could remove the sword. At one point, several of them even got the notion to tie the sword pommel to a few of their horses and pull it loose as they'd seen the serfs in the farmland below do to uncooperative tree stumps on many occasions. This action only served to snap the rope and send both horses and riders tumbling pell-mell down the grassy slopes accompanied by the uproarious laughter of their comrades.

"They'll be about that sort of nonsense for many an hour, my dears," laughed Merlin, "Let us hie we hence to my larder for some tea."

"Ooh! Do you have any fudge?" squealed Carol, "I love fudge!"

"I know not this 'fudge' of which thou speakest, friend Carol. T' is certain we have much to learn from one another!" puzzled Merlin as he, Christmas Eve and the Sugar Plum Fairies turned and strolled merrily into the castle.

Charlie The Yeti had, at last, come face to face with his Uncle Grimfang. It just wasn't turning out to be the warm family reunion Charlie had hoped for, what with both of them being pinned down behind a watering trough, hiding from marauding hordes of Hun bandits led by the fierce Attila The Hun… a bandit horde that Charlie, himself, had led to his uncle's village.

"What are you doing here, nephew?" growled Grimfang.

"I wanted to come visit you for the holidays," started Charlie, sheepishly.

"And you brought friends!" sneered Grimfang, "How nice."

"But, but that's not how it is at all," protested Charlie as he began to weave his tale of woe concerning his theft of the Golden Garland of Zeus and his miserable misadventures in France, Transylvania and along the oriental trade routes, leading up to that very moment, pausing only sporadically in his narrative to peek over the lip of the trough in an effort to see if the Huns had ridden on and, finding that NOT to be the case, slumping back down to continue his story.

"And did it never occur to you that stealing from Santa Claus might end badly?" scoffed Uncle Grimfang.

"You never were the shiniest apple on the family tree, boy, and this latest escapade is proof positive of that little fact!"

"Uncle! That really hurts, coming from you," mewled Charlie, "I thought I was your favorite!"

"Favorite from a distance," jeered Grimfang, "Why do you think when the Tibetan Yetis decided to relocate to The Fade, I leapt at the chance? Relatives are like spit... a necessary evil and best digested when swallowed in small amounts stretched out over a long period of time!"

Charlie was stunned! All these years he'd painted a mental picture of his uncle as a nurturing familial patriarch. In fact, that thought was one of the only things that got Charlie through some of his darkest, loneliest days on Bittercold Mountain. No matter how wretched and melancholy his life might be, there was always Uncle Grimfang; good ol' Uncle Grimfang and his letters regaling Charlie with ribald stories of life in Tibet; dear Uncle Grimfang and his small gifts every Christmas; Uncle Grimfang... the colossal JERK!

"Fine!" spat Charlie, "I won't 'bother' you any more than I have to. I'm going home!"

"Ooh! Ooh! Charlie's going home! Charlie's feelings are hurt!" mocked Grimfang, "And how, pray tell, are you going to manage that, boy?"

"Why, I'll just…" started Charlie.

Dang! Uncle Grimfang was right! Charlie was in no position to extricate himself from behind the trough, let alone starting the arduous trek back to the North Pole. Not without help, anyway. Charlie surmised that he needed his uncle's assistance regardless of his current anger and shame. But the only way to gain the old reprobate's aid, Charlie deduced, was to help his uncle out of their current predicament first.

"No…" effused Charlie, clearing his throat for effect, "It wouldn't be right to leave you here in these dire straits, Uncle! I shall simply have to rescue you from those marauding invaders!"

"No, that's okay, boy," replied Grimfang with just a tinge of suspicion in his voice, "The brigands seem to be dispersing. I'll be all right. You run along, now. Don't let me keep you."

Grimfang knew that Charlie was up to something self-serving and underhanded. That's what he'd do in a similar circumstance and he, Grimfang, did teach Charlie everything he knew about backstabbing and betrayal. It was an uncle's duty, after all. Charlie's brow furrowed at his relative's obstinacy.

"No, no, Uncle," Charlie submitted, "This mess is partially my doing…"

"It's ALL your doing!" chortled Grimfang.

"You say to-MAY-to, I say to-MAH-to." Charlie shot back, "In any case, I feel responsible for your safety. Tell you what, I'll help YOU get back to your home unscathed and you help ME get my horse back and some food and drink for my long trip back to the North Pole. Deal?"

"Okay," replied Grimfang.

Charlie was staggered. That worked? Either he was getting much better at lying or his uncle was much more of a dullard than Charlie had hoped. Regardless of which, Charlie was going to get his way and that was just fine, thought the beleaguered Yeti. Looking up from behind the trough, Charlie noted a lull in the action and, grabbing his uncle firmly by the scruff of the neck, leapt up and began open field running from building to building in a serpentine pattern, dragging his uncooperative relative behind him.

After some minutes of this, Charlie paused behind a fence on the outskirts of the other side of town, several hundred yards from Uncle Grimfang's hovel at the edge of the steep mountain hillside. He looked furtively from side to side and prepared to make the last hundred yard sprint to his uncle's house when Uncle Grimfang spoke up.

"Wait, boy! Attila The Hun knows why you've come to our village and may be lying in wait for you inside! Better let me go in first," whispered Charlie's uncle.

"Oh, no you don't!" rasped Charlie, "I'm not letting you go in there and leave me out here in the open all alone!"

"In that case," said Grimfang, looking around for some solution to this impasse and spying two large rain barrels, "Let's hide in those rain barrels until dark and look to see if there's any movement inside my house from a safe hiding place."

Uncle Grimfang sauntered cautiously across the yard to the barrels and, looking left and right for any signs of Hunnish activity, started to climb into the one nearest the lip of the hillside.

"Not so fast," murmured Charlie, "I'll take that barrel!"

Charlie was beginning to get an uneasy feeling about his uncle and seeing Grimfang's eagerness for that one, particular barrel, decided that if Uncle Grimfang were planning some sort of ambush he, Charlie, would not want to be in the wrong barrel. No, sir. Charlie wasn't born yesterday! Charlie had no sooner wedged himself tightly within the confines of the barrel, however, than Uncle Grimfang's massive right foot gave the cask a swift punt over the hillside.

As Charlie's barrel tumbled over the precipice down the long mountain ledge to the valley far, far below, gaining momentum with every rotation, Uncle Grimfang made a capital letter "L" with his right thumb and index finger and held it firmly against his own forehead, signifying his disdain for his "loser" relative.

"Merry Christmas, nephew!" Grimfang smiled as Charlie barreled down the mountainside out of sight.

END CHAPTER TEN

Chapter Eleven

As Charlie's barrel gained momentum down the Himalayan slopes, spinning faster and faster with each bumpy revolution, the harassed yeti's brain whirled in a frenzy of delirium, first dizziness, then nausea until, finally, Charlie blacked out altogether.

It was just as well. Through some miracle of happenstance, the barrel didn't smash to bits against the rocks, nor did it plunge off any cliffs to hurtle towards a demolishing end on a jagged stone bed. No, quite to the contrary, the barrel rolled and bounced from snow covered path to heather lined mountain trail, gradually slowing as it spun and jostled wildly through wheat fields, cow pastures and sheep meadows until, fortuitously, it clattered along cobbled streets into a small valley town and came to an abrupt splintering halt when it met up with an imposing and unyielding manure heap next to the town's train depot.

Charlie awoke from his unconscious state to the incessant buzzing of horse flies and a rancorous odor that seemed to infuse the very follicles of his massive, hairy frame. As he attempted to focus his watering eyes, he noticed several young street urchins standing nearby, watching him and giggling with delight.

"Do it again!" shouted one boy in ragged pants and bare feet.

"That was awesome!" cried another, wearing a battered fez.

"Phew! You really stink, mister!" chimed in a young girl wearing a head scarf.

"Where am I..?" questioned Charlie.

"Constantinople!" chimed the children in unison, "Everybody knows that!"

Charlie sat amidst the manure and splintered wood that once was his "hiding" barrel and tried to put all the pieces together. The last thing he remembered was his Uncle's voice, saying something about Christmas while growing fainter and more distant. He wasn't sure, but Charlie surmised that his old Uncle Grimfang had just pulled a fast one on him. Regardless, Charlie seemed not much worse for wear, physically, and his uncle's antics DID provide him with a way out of his pact with Attila The Hun. It also seemed that Charlie's rollicking ride had taken him into another area of The Fade entirely, well away from the commotion of the Mountain Yeti village. Not a bad turn of events, mused the stench-ridden yeti.

As he stood up and shook large clumps of manure from his fur, Charlie's size and demeanor frightened the children and they ran off towards town, wailing at the top of their lungs about the "stinky monster".

"Oh, great!" spat Charlie, "That's all I need… MORE villagers with pitchforks and torches!"

Charlie looked around for a hiding place and spied a water tower next to the train tracks, just to the left of the luggage platform for the depot. Thinking to kill two birds with one stone, hiding out AND washing away the malodorous stench of the manure, Charlie furtively inched along the building, trying to stay in the shadows provided by the roof overhang, climbed the tower with all the apelike agility he could muster and slid quietly into the cold water of the trough.

Charlie bobbed silently inside the water tower, listening to the voices of the townspeople who had followed the children back to the remains of his barrel. There was much milling about and yelling for a long time and, on several occasions, Charlie feared that he'd be discovered, hearing the voices directly beneath him as they followed the tracks, checking in the boxcars that sat idle on side tracks and in the roundhouse. The villagers never thought to look up at the water tower, however, and, after a time, the impromptu posse dispersed, chastising the youngsters for wasting their time with such childish nonsense as "stinky monsters".

"What now?" thought Charlie to himself as he bobbed soundlessly in the frigid water, "My toes are starting to prune up."

Christmas Eve and Merlin were enjoying their tea and scones, though Merlin was a tad vexed that Carol couldn't explain how to make fudge with exacting enough details that would allow the aged sorcerer to conjure some up. Carol, like her sisters Holly and Noel, had given up on trying to school Merlin on the finer points of confectioner's sugar and had, instead, taken to playing a game of pick-up sticks on the cold marble floor of Merlin's quarters with a young page named Arthur.

"And that's the whole, sad story, Mr. Merlin," Eve said, ending the tale of how she and the girls came to be in his portion of The Fade, "We've simply got to retrieve the Golden Garland of Zeus before Santa has to make his yearly ride or Christmas will be in shambles."

"To say nothing of a yeti running willy-nilly across The Fade," chirped Merlin between sips of tea, "There be a precarious peace betwixt some of the regions herein and 't would accomplish naught but ill for all for this Charlie scoundrel to upset that delicate balance. My contacts in the spirit world already whisper of a bloody altercation between the Tibetan Mountain yetis and Attila's rampaging Huns."

"Fear ye not, fair Eve," Merlin continued, "Old though I may be, still dost I possess faculties enow to spirit you and your companions to the general vicinity of your long sought quarry.”

Gathering the Sugar Plum Fairies close around her at Merlin‘s bidding, Christmas Eve stood inside a hastily drawn chalk circle in the center of the room.

“T’ will be but a moment’s thing, dear lady, and my charm shall hie thee hence to wherever Charlie be. Hence, I say!” trilled Merlin.

As the wizened magician proceeded to summon the necessary incantations to mind, a small commotion erupted from outside his window in the sward below. The knights and squires who had been trying to remove the sword from the cleft of the rock where Eve had thrust it were fast becoming frustrated with the seemingly impossible task and their aggravation was taking its toll on their spirit of cooperation. Taking turns became more frantic and far less fair. A line jumping nudge led to a push, which led to a jostle, which in turn led to a shove, followed in short order by hitting, swearing and cudgel brandishing. Soon, outright brawling erupted amidst the gathered throng.

“Oh, fie!” spat Merlin, “How is a wizard to concentrate with all that brouhaha befouling the tranquility of the day!? Arthur! Be a stout lad and fetch me that sword so that I may conjure in quiet! Go, boy!”

“At once, M’ lord,” replied the smallish page, rising from the floor and scampering down the spiral stairway leading from Merlin’s tower to the castle keep below.

“Merlin!” cried Eve, “That skinny little boy will never be able to pull that sword out of that boulder!”

“Shh!” scolded Merlin, “What he knows not shall ne’er do him harm!”

Then, with a sly twinkle in his rheumy eye, Merlin gesticulated several arcane signs in the air and Eve and the girls began to vanish.

"Give my regards to the druids," chuckled Merlin as, after watching the girls fade away completely, he turned towards his window and the collective gasps of astonishment echoing from the court-yard below.

Henry Cobbler's heart raced as he crested the hill just beyond the old haunted grist mill. He'd never seen a yeti before. Truth be told, Henry had never seen a bear up close before, either. Henry wasn't much for camping or the great outdoors and, in all his time at St. Augustus' Orphanage in Lancastershire, there had never been so much as a hint of a field trip to a zoo, so he wasn't quite sure which it was that had treed Ferret Reynolds and Guinevere Upington-Smythe.

"Bless my stars and garters," gasped Henry, "That's a right plight my chums are in!"

As Henry hunkered down in the tall grass, trying for all the world not to be seen by the hulking brute menacing his friends, all his druidic lessons tumbled through his brain at once, jockeying for position as the BEST way to deal with this current situation. Henry scrambled on his elbows, commando style, to his left as the words "stay downwind, don't let him catch a whiff of you, stay downwind" echoed through his mind. Reaching his desired leeward position on the ridge, Henry regained a sitting position and began running druidic incantations through his mind.

"I suppose it DOES make a difference if the creature is a bear or a yeti," Henry mused, "Still, one hairy brute is much the same as another when it comes to spells that hurl large rocks or open yawning chasms beneath one's feet. I'm only second year. I don't know any of those sorts of USEFUL enchantments. It's a downright shame that my mates aren't being menaced by a turtle that needs turning purple! I'd give the bounder what for then, I'll wager."

Henry's reverie was interrupted by a piercing shriek. The yeti had grabbed Guinevere by the ankle and was attempting to pull her downward. Ferret held tightly to Gwen's arm with one hand and, legs braced between branches of a fork in the tree trunk, pelted the hairy man brute with leaves and acorns with his free hand, all the while shouting epithets such as "Boo-yah!" "Hey, hey!" and "Bad doggy!" at the beast.

"It's now or never!" barked Henry, trying to screw up his courage for a desperate lunge at the monster with a pointy stick he'd found on the ground nearby. As the boy slunk closer to the predetermined position he would make his charge from, a quote from one of his personal heroes, Winston Churchill, rang in his ears.

"Although prepared for martyrdom, I preferred that it be postponed!" shouted Henry as he leapt to his feet brandishing his wooden weapon over his head and tearing pell-mell down the slope towards the tree lined clearing.

It was at that precise moment that a magnificent flash of light engulfed the entire area, blinding everyone, including Henry. As the erstwhile rescuer tripped over his own stick and began tumbling head over heels down the lush hillock, the last thing he heard before sweet oblivion engulfed him was a woman's voice yelling "Charlie! Leave those children alone!"

END CHAPTER ELEVEN

Chapter Twelve

Charlie the Yeti bobbed lazily in the water tower for what seemed like weeks but was, in fact, little more than a half hour. Still, the frigid waters took their toll on the hirsute misanthrope, leaving him with stiff, aching joints and prune wrinkled feet. When Charlie had made sure that the townspeople had given up the search for their children's "monster" and gone back to their normal activities, he slowly, achingly hoisted himself out of the water tower and hobbled off behind the ticket office of the train depot.

"Gee, it's just like home… only wetter!" groused Charlie, trying to regain circulation in his legs by vigorously rubbing them with his massive hands, spraying icy water on the weather beaten boards of the ticket office. As he crouched down behind the building, glancing furtively from side to side, striving to avoid detection, Charlie heard voices from inside the depot.

"The main line is clear and the boiler's stoked. We're ready to debark." came one of the voices.

"Very good," chimed the other, "The Orient Express from Constantinople to London has never run late and it never will on my watch!"

"Orient Express to London? What a stroke of luck," thought Charlie, incredulously. The harried yeti had long since made up his mind that his holiday visit to his Uncle Grimfang was an ill-conceived debacle at best, and the most prudent thing for him was to cut his losses and go back home to Bittercold Mountain. The only obstacle was in how to get there without all the slogging through swamps and skulking across the different hostile regions of The Fade that his trip thus far had presented him.

Peering out from the shadows at the side of the roundhouse, Charlie saw The Orient Express, gleaming like a new penny, sitting on the tracks of the main line, chugging black plumes of smoke into the darkening sky. The wily yeti watched the rail yard security guards walking up and down both sides of the locomotive while porters loaded luggage and sacks of mail aboard the Baggage Car set near the rear of the train, just two cars up from the caboose. Charlie made careful calculations of the guards' rounds using the "one Mississippi, two Mississippi" method of counting. It wouldn't do for him to be seen (and possibly clubbed) at this juncture, when he was so close to his goal.

After about a quarter hour or so, Charlie was confident in the guards' pattern and when they would be at the opposite ends of the train. Waiting for just that precise moment, Charlie bolted out from between buildings and dove under the train in a nimble tuck and roll. He lay there, hugging track and silently counting out his Mississippi's until he was sure the guards were once again at opposite ends of the train. Then, he crawled up into the undercarriage and wedged himself in tightly between the axles and the floor of the car above him. Pulling out the Golden Garland from his lederhosen, Charlie lashed his torso to several iron cross bars.

"This infernal swag is finally doing its job," snarked Charlie, "Helping me gain free passage from one area of The Fade to another!"

Charlie heard the conductor call "all aboard" and, within the space of a few minutes, the train lurched into motion. Though it was a jarring lurch, the finely crafted golden garland held firm and Charlie the Yeti was on his way, his triumphant laughter drowned out by the escaping steam and clickety clacking of the wheels along the tracks.

The last few miles of Charlie's trip from Constantinople to London seemed the most interminable. He had traveled freely from one region of The Fade to another, lashed to the under carriage of The Orient Express -- one of the few conveyances in the whole of The Fade that could claim free passage from one area to another with little consequence -- but these last several leagues, with their big city sounds and smells just wore on the luckless yeti's spirits.

"Aw, c'mon!" griped Charlie, "Won't this ride EVER end?" My fingers are numb and the garland is rubbing away the fur around my hips. I just want to get OFF!"

As if in answer to Charlie's plaintive wailing, the great, gleaming locomotive began slowing down until the squealing metal on metal noise of the brakes being applied set Charlie's teeth on end. London, at last! Now it would be only a hop, skip and jump to the frozen north and home!

"'Bout time," sighed Charlie, who then proceeded to wait the better part of an hour, still roped to the iron framework of the train's underbelly, for the passengers to debark and luggage and mail to be unloaded. When the crafty yeti determined that all activity surrounding his hiding berth had ceased, he clumsily, with ice-encrusted claws, untied the Golden Garland of Zeus, dropping to the track bed with an unceremonious plop. After kissing the cold earth several times in grateful affection and stretching his limbs in an effort to regain his "land legs" and settle the bump and rattle that had permeated his very being, Charlie glanced about and, seeing no one, bolted for the shadows of Victorian London.

Henry Cobbler had dreamed of many frightening and wondrous things in his young life; dragons and witches and spacemen with laser pistols. He'd dreamt of battling sinister bunnies atop the St. Louis Arch and pie fights with zebras along the Great Wall of China. He'd spent many a slumbering night in the company of kings, commoners, villains and Hollywood starlets. None of these, however, could've prepared Henry for what he was seeing as he awoke from his unconscious state amidst the scrub grass on the hillside.

"Blimey! I've visions of Sugar Plums dancing in my head!" exclaimed Henry, bolting upright and adjusting his glasses.

"We're not dancing," shrugged Holly.

"Better get those Coke bottles checked, kid," smirked Noel.

"I can dance if you want. Do you know 'I'm A Little Teapot'?" offered Carol.

"Girls, give the boy some room," came Christmas Eve's voice from some distance away.

At the sound of the soothing voice, Henry jerked his head to the left and saw Christmas Eve standing atop a hogtied Charlie the Yeti. Charlie was snarling and snapping at a giddy Ferret Reynolds, who was capering about Charlie's prostrate form, poking him with a branch from the very tree Charlie had just moments ago had him and Guinevere Upington-Smythe trapped in.

"Oi've got yer now, ye great big yeti, you!" crowed Ferret Reynolds, unconcerned with the fact that it was Christmas Eve who actually subdued the hapless hairy beast and not he.

"B-but how..?" Henry stammered, rubbing his eyes in disbelief and adjusting his glasses for a better view of the tableau unfolding before him.

"HA! What f'r you, 'Enry Cobbler!" boasted the ebullient Reynolds, "whose idea was it to bring the bull rope which now ties up the ruddy beast? Mine! That's who! And you said it wouldn't work!"

"I never said…" returned Henry, choosing to judiciously put aside for the moment that the rope was, in fact, NOT used in the manner

Reynolds had intended and no yeti snare was in evidence.

"Stop stammering, Henry Cobbler! You sound like a motor boat on the Mersey," interjected Guinevere, "just admit that Ferret was right all along!"

Christmas Eve stood silently by as the teens squabbled amongst themselves. Finally, she cleared her throat and spoke up.

"Children! I'm not sure what's going on here or why Charlie was attacking you, but we've come a long way to retrieve the…"

Eve paused and looked around the dappled glen for some hint of the Golden Garland, yet saw no sign of the fabled swag.

"Where is it, Charlie? Where's the garland?" scolded Christmas Eve, holding Charlie upside down and shaking him vigorously.

"He doesn't have it, Eve!" mewled Holly.

"It's nowhere around here," added Noel.

"The rapscallion has absconded with the loot!" chimed Carol.

"My friend, Mr. Holmes taught me that saying," she continued with a giggle.

Indeed, it seemed that Carol's assessment was correct. Some-how, during the melee, Charlie had lost the garland and there was no way of determining exactly where, in the general area, it was. The fairies flitted willy-nilly around the vicinity of the grist mill, look-ing under rocks, in tree boughs, and skimming the pool with long sticks, but to no avail. The three Stonehenge Academy students had no idea what they were looking for, Ferret and Guinevere having been up a tree with their eyes shut in terror and Henry Cob-bler busy rolling down a hill into unconsciousness. Christmas Eve was fast becoming vexed.

"It's got to be around SOMEWHERE," spoke an exasperated Eve,

"It's a glimmering golden Christmas swag. It shouldn't be THAT hard to find."

"No, it shouldn't," came a cold, commanding voice from the edge of a copse of hemlock trees off to the east of the glen, "at least as easy as finding four Christmas TRESPASSERS and a hogtied yeti!"

Standing in the clearing was a lithe, imposing figure with a short scraggly beard and piercing azure blue eyes. He wore an ankle length tunic, festooned with archaic runes that looked as though it were fashioned from burlap. A wreath of woven hawthorn branches encircled his bald head. In his left hand, he held a set of eight point deer antlers and in his right hand he gripped a gnarled staff made from holly boughs. This was Headmaster Fraxineus. He was accompanied by Custodian Homberg, a portly man in hunter green leggings, a well-worn khaki canvas cap and a dull leather tunic. He sported a bushy beard that was interwoven with many small bits of shrubbery and twigs. Neither looked particularly happy to find a coterie of their hated Christmas enemies running free on the grounds of Stonehenge Academy. Fraxineus held up a gnarled staff in his right, robed hand and cleared his throat.

"Homberg, take custody of the yeti. Children, return to your respective dormitories immediately! You four will come with me, now!" barked the headmaster authoritatively.

"I bagged the beastie, Homberg," interjected Ferret Reynolds as the Custodian hefted the still bound Charlie up by the scruff of his neck, "any reward should be mine!"

"Virtue… and NOT being expelled, is its own reward, young trainee," replied Homberg sardonically.

"Wheee! There's going to be a council trial!" squealed Guinevere with unbridled glee, "these Christmas criminals are in for it, now!"

Henry Cobbler, who rather liked Christmas in the first place and saw no malice in the visitors' actions heretofore in the second, was not one bit happy at this turn of events and, judging by the looks on

the faces of Eve and the fairies, neither were his new acquaintanc-
es.

END CHAPTER TWELVE

Chapter Thirteen

Charlie The Yeti had never had a bubble bath before. Point of fact, Charlie had never had what one would call a "bath" at all. Yetis seemed to prefer the pungent, aromatic natural scent that living in caves provided and, as far as washing away grime, well, that's what rain was for, after all. Yet, there sat Charlie in a large hammered cast iron tub, lathered up from head to toe and being scrubbed down by several of Custodian Homberg's assistants.

Off to one side, Charlie saw his lederhosen, mended, pressed and neatly laid out for him, along with his Alpine hat, steamed and blocked with a bright, new cardinal feather protruding jauntily from the band. Charlie was being made presentable for future inclusion in the Stonehenge Academy Menagerie and the truth of it was, Charlie very much enjoyed the pampering treatment! After all, what was there not to like? Three square meals a day, a fairly temperate habitat far away from the keening winds and ice caves of Bittercold Mountain and all Charlie had to do was loll around his enclosure all day, snarl regularly and occasionally lunge at the first years, scaring them into soiling themselves, much to the delight of the upper classmen.

"Finally," Charlie mused to himself while absentmindedly blowing suds into the air and watching them dissipate into minute sparkling rainbows, "Good ol' Charlie has landed in the clover!"

As Charlie closed his eyes and hunkered down in the tub, waiting for the assistants to pour in another bucket of hot water, his mind wandered into reverie, ticking off the events of the day that had led him to his current situation.

After leaving the train depot, Charlie wandered footsore across the English countryside, looking for some sustenance, maybe a pie carelessly left on a windowsill, just right for the filching. Finding none, Charlie continued ever north, growing more sour with every mile. He certainly was not in the mood to deal with a pair of cater-wauling sprouts with a bull rope. Enough was enough, Charlie reasoned, and he gave chase to Ferret and Guinevere, cornering them up a sycamore tree.

"And that's when those busybodies from Christmas Valley showed up to spoil my fun," murmured Charlie, "Looking for that infernal garland! Well, it did me very little good while in my possession, so I hope they NEVER find it and if they do, I hope they CHOKE on it!"

Charlie grew agitated at the thought of Christmas Eve and the Sugar Plum fairies and, forgetting where he was for the moment, clapped his hands together defiantly, splashing water and suds onto the floor and over Homberg's assistants, drenching everything within a ten foot radius.

"Towels, lackeys!" roared Charlie, "And be quick about it! I'm starting to prune! And I'm anxious to learn the fate of those stupid Christmas meddlers!"

Christmas Eve tested the strength of the bars of her cage for the tenth time and found them just as durable as they were her first nine attempts. The dank dungeon prison smelled like fetid moss and moldy straw, a stench which assaulted her senses and only served to punctuate her and the girls' dire situation. They were in the custody of their avowed enemies, the Druids, and, without the safe passage provided by the Golden Garland of Zeus, they had no recourse to escape their current plight.

"What's going to happen to us, Eve?" wept Holly.

"I betcha we get the chair… ZAP!" snarked Noel'

"Couldn't they just overload us with fudge until we burst? I wouldn't mind going that way," cooed Carol, smacking her lips.

"Calm down, girls," Eve replied in a soothing tone, "I'm sure if we could just talk to someone in charge, explain our reasons for being here, they'd understand and let us go. We mean them no harm, after all."

"That's probably not going to happen," came a voice from outside their cell, "The Druids have no love lost for anything having to do with Christmas!"

It was Henry Cobbler, cleaned and bandaged from his tumble down the hill earlier. Henry was curious about the visitors from Christmas Valley and wanted a chance to talk with them so, in spite of Headmaster Fraxineus' admonition to the contrary, risking detention or worse, Henry had snuck out of his dorm room and furtively made his way to the dungeon holding cells.

"Hullo! My name is Henry Cobbler and I'm a second year here at Stonehenge Academy, but I'm not like the others. I was raised by Celtlings."

"Celtlings?" queried Eve.

"Regular people. Not Druids." replied Henry.

"Oh! Like us," offered Holly.

"Oh, no! Nothing like you, Miss!" continued Henry, "You're Christmas folk and even though the Druids tolerate Celtlings, they have much animosity towards anyone and anything connected to Christmas!"

"Why? What'd we ever do to them?" huffed Noel.

"Are Celtlings like ducklings?" added Carol "Everybody likes ducklings!"

Henry Cobbler paused and scratched his head, not knowing quite what to make of the little pink fairy but knowing that she did make him smile. He very much liked that. After a few moments, Henry composed himself and related the whole sad history of the Druid-Christian "feud" and the co-opting of the Winter Solstice and the ensuing generations of inbred enmity for the celebrants of the Christmas holidays.

"They're like as not going to put you on trial and set an example for anyone "Christmassy" who might have the audacity to invade their sovereignty in the future," warned Henry.

"Can you help us, Henry?" asked Eve.

"I don't know about that, Miss! I'm likely to be in a right plight myself if anyone catches me even talking to you… but, how can I help?"

"If you could only find the garland," started Eve but was interrupted by the sound of scuffling feet and keys turning in rusty locks.

"I dunno, Miss…" sputtered Henry, "If I… I… I can't… I've got to go!"

Henry Cobbler crouched down and dislodged a largish flagstone near the base of the far wall of the dungeon corridor, revealing a hidden tunnel, scurried in, pulling the flagstone closed behind him, and was gone just as Headmaster Fraxineus, flanked by two imposing druidic guards, entered the prison cell area.

"I hope you've enjoyed your stay in our fine dungeon accommodations," oiled Fraxineus, "But the time has come to put Christmas on trial! Bind them!"

Henry Cobbler peeked out of the tunnel from behind the flagstone in time to see Christmas Eve, hands bound tightly, and the Sugar Plum Fairies, stuffed into three medium sized bird cages, being led off down the corridor by the guards.

"Take them to the Council Ring!" barked Fraxineus.

"Oh, whatever am I going to do now?" sobbed Henry.

END CHAPTER THIRTEEN

Chapter Fourteen

The Salisbury Amphitheater was indeed a sight to behold. Opulent in scope without being pretentious, its rough-hewn stone gallery was positioned in a semi-circular fashion facing the massive dais which, though no one wanted to admit it, was more than likely used for human sacrifice in the ancient days of the druidic sect. The amphitheater was ringed by monolithic stone columns, etched with arcane sigils and topped with enormous stone slabs so that it closely resembled the actual Stonehenge located on England's Salisbury plains, for which it was named. Off to the left of the dais in a small portico stood a small man-sized arch that resembled the much larger capped columns that encircled the amphitheater. This was Stonehenge Academy's entrance-exit to The Fade.

Christmas Eve thought how easy it would be to snap the ropes binding her wrists and "bolt for the door", putting an end to this nonsense were it not for the facts that she STILL didn't have the Golden Garland of Zeus that she was sent to retrieve AND that Holly, Noel and Carol were yet imprisoned in their three respective bird cages.

"We'll just have to see this through, girls," she reassured the fairies, "Don't give up hope! There's always a chance!"

"Maybe they'll grant us clemency," added Holly, secretly satisfied with herself for using such a big word as "clemency" correctly.

"We're bustin' out at midnight, see?" interjected Noel trying to lighten the mood, "No two-bit slammer can hold Machine Gun Noel, see?"

"WRAAARK! WRAAAK! Carol wants a cracker!" added Carol, hopping around her cage and flapping her arms, pretending to be a parrot.

The four captives' banter stopped, however, when a hush fell over the arena as the entire student body of Stonehenge Academy marched purposefully to the gallery, silently taking their seats. When all were seated, the druid who was the proceeding's Sergeant-At-Arms lit the braziers on either side if the dais and announced the tribunal that would sit in judgement over the "Christmas criminals".

The first to enter and take his place on the dais, of course, was Headmaster Fraxineus, now wearing a different robe than before, black with a hood and a blood red stole covered with gold sigils and runes. He was followed close behind by a similarly dressed Custodian Homberg. Finally, two more faculty members came to the pulpit, both dressed in the requisite black hooded robe and red stole.

The first was the school's verbal historian and natural sciences professor, Excentrus Dowergoth, a stern looking, slightly built man with sharp pointed features and brown glowering eyes. He was trailed by Stonehenge's meteorological and martyrdom professor (and the faculty disciplinarian), "He Whose Name Cannot Be Spoken". This was a moniker given him by some upper classmen several years prior. There was nothing singularly sinister about it. His actual name was Llewellyn Magellan Quirinius McMillan and it wasn't a name that tripped lightly off the tongue. Most of the faculty just called him "Lou". Lou had a pug nose, flaccid jowls, squinty hazel eyes and uneven yellowish teeth. But, thanks mostly to his high position in the druid community and his knowledge of obscure druidic love potions, Lou was quite a hit with the ladies at the academy's monthly bacchanalia.

The Sergeant-At-Arms raised his hands and quieted the murmuring crowd. Headmaster Fraxineus rose, sounded a small gong and cleared his throat.

"These unfortunate wretches were found trespassing on school property and openly flaunting forbidden Christmas symbols in front of several second year initiates," he opined haughtily, "Let them now present such defense as they can muster before we pass judgement!"

"Guilty! Guilty!" rose the chant from the assemblage, attaining volume and passion with each passing moment.

"That can't be good," whispered Christmas Eve.

Santa Claus stared pensively at his ornate desk calendar. It was December Twenty-third and Christmas Eve and the Sugar Plum Fairies had been gone for a day and a half. Not much time for the task assigned her, to be sure, but Saint Nicholas was quite familiar with the whimsies of The Fade. A day and a half here in the "real" world could be weeks, months, maybe even YEARS in the environs of that timeless realm, he mused. Worry etched his normally jolly face.

Santa tried to distract himself by helping out down at the reindeer stables, but he just couldn't keep his mind on the task at hand. At one point, Tinselbottom had to tactfully explain to Santa that he had put Blitzen's harness on Vixen (who was half Blitzen's girth) and he was creating more work for the groom elves than was necessary. These sorts of befuddled antics continued all day, at the toy work-shop, at the candy confectioners, until finally, Mrs. Claus had to shoo Santa out of her kitchen and back to his office, admonishing him to stay put and out of everyone's hair.
So, what could he do, then, but wait and hope that Eve and the girls were up to the challenge he'd put before them? She was a

superhero, after all. Superheroes ALWAYS come through in the clutch. Santa pinned all his hopes on that as the minutes continued to tick away.

"C'mon, Eve! Christmas is depending on you!"

Henry Cobbler was torn. He was a second year druid and an A-plus student. He had a real knack for the druidic arts and had become rather comfortable in his new life at Stonehenge Academy. On the other hand, his formative years among the Celtlings had given him a perspective unlike most of his classmates and instructors. He knew Christmas as they never could, without prejudice or preconceived rancor. Co-opting the Solstice was an ill-starred event, to be sure, but that was then, this is now. There seems to be no malice towards the druids nor slight intended. In fact, Christmas as a whole seems to embrace joy and peace and love, many of the same tenets the druids themselves espouse.

"I'd very much like to aid Christmas Eve and her friends," Henry pondered to himself, "But do I dare risk my place here at the academy and the few friends I've made along the way?"

Henry spoke, of course, of his best mate, Ferret Reynolds, and the ever exquisite Guinevere Uppington-Smythe. Even though his current relations with the pair were strained at best, Henry still considered them his best friends. The current love triangle they were embroiled in would certainly work itself out before long, especially since Ferret seemed oblivious to Gwen's noticeable advances and come hither glances.

"Perhaps," considered Henry, "I should gingerly consult my friends on the issue and come to some sort of consensus decision."

Ferret Reynolds was hunkered down on his bunk, tossing tiny

pebbles at a tin can across the room when Henry entered. He was almost sure that the sour look on Ferret's face had little to do with the fact that he was missing the can with every pebble.

"H'it h'isn't fair, 'Enry Cobbler!" Ferret whined, "H'it were my idea to go hunting the yeti and my bull rope wot ensnared the bounder! But, do I get the hinted at reward? No! A grounding, a swat on me bottom and Bob's y'r uncle f'r me troubles, thank you very much! I deserve some respiration!"

Henry wasn't sure if Ferret meant to say "restitution" or "reparations" but decided not to press the matter. He stared at his shoes and cleared his throat,

"Ahem! Yes. Quite right, Ferret, old chap! No one deserves it more than you. But, uh, what do you think about, um, Christmas Eve and the Sugar Plum Fairies, eh?"

"Wot? That bird in red an' green and her three multi-colored munchkin friends?" queried Ferret, "Right comely f'r a Celtling, I suppose, but she's doomed, of course!"

"What makes you say that, Ferret?" asked Henry.

"Cor blimey, 'Enry! She's all dolled up in Christmas regalia, h'isn't she, now? Ol' Headmaster Frax don't take kindly to that sort of folderol! 'E's like to throw the book at them!" replied Ferret, gesticulating wildly.

Henry nodded and exited the room quickly, making some excuse about chores and punishment. Ferret scarcely noticed, returning focus to his rock and can game. He was of no assistance at all and Henry couldn't help but wonder what anyone, especially Guinevere, saw in the boy. Pushing those jealous thoughts to the back of his brain, Henry made his way down the creaky wooden back staircase to the girl's floor dorm rooms and his anticipated meeting with Gwen.

It was kind of eerie to find the typically bustling dorms empty thought Henry, but only he, Ferret and Gwen were confined to quarters. All the other students were at the conclave at Salisbury Amphitheater, sitting in judgement over his new Christmas friends. As he approached Gwen's room, he was more confounded than ever. He hoped Gwen's normally sensible mind and frank manner could give him some much needed clarity.

"Good old down-to-earth Gwen," thought Henry, "She'll give me some rational advice! She's not given to flights of fancy like Ferret!"

As Henry approached Gwen's room, he noticed the door slightly ajar and heard giggling and singing coming from inside. As he drew closer and cautiously pushed the door ever more slightly open, he saw Guinevere dancing in front of her full length mirror and singing "I Feel Pretty". As he opened the door wider and made a slight noise to alert her to his presence, Henry was thunderstruck by what he saw. Gwen was dancing and singing in front of her mirror, wearing the Golden Garland of Zeus like a feathered boa!

Headmaster Fraxineus motioned for silence from the students and faculty in the gallery seating. The crowd reluctantly quelled their exuberant chanting and fell silent save for a few whispers and murmurs scattered throughout the council ring, accompanied by disapproving shushes.

"Some background is in order," began Fraxineus, "so that the accused may fully understand the enormity of their crimes. To that end, I call upon Excentrus Dowergoth to recite the Druid Chronicles!"

An audible groan could be heard coming from the Fourth Years. Druid culture foregoes the writing down of events in their history, opting instead for an oral tradition. It began that way centuries ago when they were forbidden by law to do so and it has since become ritual practice. In any event, Dowergoth's droning voice was said to put the very stones to sleep and the Fourth Years had heard his dissertations many, many times before. The first and second year students were in for a treat, a baptism by fire of sorts. The Fourth Years just decided a nap was in order. It was going to be a long afternoon.

END CHAPTER FOURTEEN

Chapter Fifteen

Christmas Eve sat cross-legged on the cold stone floor, head in hand. Holly played with her ponytail, attempting to braid the parts of it she could reach. Noel paced her cage like a tigress, clicking the wire bars with her finger. Carol was curled up in the corner of her cage, asleep, snoring like a chainsaw. The sun was beginning to sink low on the horizon and Excentrus Dowergoth was only now beginning to wind down his treatise on "The Great Affront" and the co-opting of the Winter Solstice by benign, but imprudent Christians several hundreds of years ago.

Eve was beginning to understand. She, as The First Lady of Yuletide Cheer and a goodwill ambassador for the Christmas season, was a slight to the druids solely based on her festive appearance. This was an enmity that went back generations and there was little she could do to dissuade her captors of the notion that she and the girls were here to steal even more of their proud culture. Eve stood and faced the tribunal.

"If I may speak," started Eve,

"You may NOT!" fired back Headmaster Fraxineus, "your time for rebuttal will come AFTER the formal charges have been read and witnesses have been deposed!"

"But, sir…" Eve pleaded.

"Bailiff, gag the defendant!" spat "He Whose Name Cannot Be Spoken", Llewellyn Magellan Quirinius McMillan (a.k.a. Lou), who was just rousing from the stupor he'd fallen into during Excentrus Dowergoth's dissertation, "these proceedings will be carried out in an orderly manner in accordance to our laws! We will brook no untoward interruptions."

A leather strap was fastened securely over Christmas Eve's mouth, rendering further protestations unlikely. The Sugar Plum Fairies were about to object when they noticed three additional leather straps lying next to the dais and thought better of it.

"We will now consider motive," continued Fraxineus, seemingly oblivious of the kerfuffle of minutes earlier, "for that, I turn the proceedings over to Custodian Homberg."

A murmur of approval echoed through the gallery. Most all the student body and faculty loved the grizzled groundskeeper's down to earth demeanor. Homberg quieted the crowd with a slight wave of his hand.

"For my first witness," bellowed Homberg, "I call forward Stonehenge Academy's newest zoological acquisition, Charlie The Yeti!"

As Charlie took his place on the dais, Eve shot him a glance that spoke volumes more than her gagged mouth ever could.

Henry Cobbler could scarcely believe his eyes! There stood Guinevere, sweet, beautiful Guinevere, the sum of all his desires, wearing the very golden swag she had insisted, just hours before, that she had absolutely no knowledge of! Henry was perplexed. Could Gwen, lovely, demure Gwen have lied? How unlike her! In all the time he had known her, Henry had found her to be the paragon of frank honesty! He needed to investigate further.

"That's a right nice scarf you have there, Gwen," Henry began cautiously, "It quite resembles the holiday swag that Christmas Eve described to us earlier… the one she was searching for. You know, the very one you swore you'd never seen or even heard of?"

"Oh, that," cooed Guinevere, "I saw it fly off into a thicket during that woman's tussle with the yeti. I thought it looked so pretty, so I scooped it up and stuffed it inside my Academy blazer.'

"But, you said…" stammered Henry, "And she needed…"

"What, then, Henry Cobbler? I should care for the likes of her?" interrupted Guinevere, "She's obviously one of those Christmas Anarchists the Headmaster is always warning us about! If she wanted this swag so badly, it's more than likely she stole it from some poor unfortunate in the first place! Turnabout is fair play, I say! Maybe she'll even learn a lesson from this incident but, being one of those Christmas ilk, I sincerely doubt it! Skullduggery is in their nature, you know!"

Henry knew no such thing. All his experiences with Christmas had been pleasant. He was pondering how he might break through Gwen's prejudice and explain, maybe by playing on her sense of gratitude (after all, Christmas Eve had saved her and Ferret from the yeti) when she continued.

"Besides, Henry, you must admit this boa certainly dresses up my drab school uniform. Ferret can't help but notice me, now!" clucked Gwen delightedly as she continued to prance and pose in front of her looking glass.

"Ah, ha!" thought Henry, "There's the heart of my argument if I play my cards right!"

Henry slyly approached Gwen again, feigning acquiescence to her position.

"Oh, I'm sure Ferret will be delighted by the golden garland, Gwen!" Henry shrewdly remarked, "Those sorts of frills generally make ol' Ferret quite giddy!"

"Oh, do you really think so, Henry?" gasped Guinevere.

"Oh, quite so, Gwen," Henry continued, "In fact, he was just lamenting the fact that such a comely maid as Christmas Eve had lost such a magnificent accessory as that. You know, one that might provide her free access back to where she came from."

"C-comely?" asked Gwen, falteringly.

"Oh, my, yes," Henry persisted craftily, "'Right comely' were his exact words, I do believe."

This was no lie, of course. Ferret HAD said those exact words, though not quite in the tone and timbre Henry implied. Nonetheless, Henry allowed Gwen to believe whatever she wished, having lost all desire and much of his respect for his friend due to her callous disdain for Christmas Eve and her friends. Why, even Charlie The Yeti deserved better than what she was willing to give.

"But, the Golden Garland is yours, now," Henry said nonchalantly, "So, I suppose those dastardly Christmas criminals will be tried, found guilty and cast into the dungeon forever, just out of reach, but never out of our minds… or hearts."

"Henry Cobbler, you're MEAN!" screeched Guinevere, "Poor, poor Ferret mustn't be forced to pine away for some unrequited fantasy love that can never be his! This Eve person must be sent away before that dear boy's momentary flirtation becomes a flaming infatuation that will break his heart and consume him!"

"Why, I never thought of it that way," replied Henry, innocently, "but what can I do?"

"You're supposed to be his friend, Henry Cobbler!" squealed Gwen, shoving the garland into Henry's arms, "You take this infernal bunting and give it right back to her and show her the door! Do it, Henry! NOW!"

"As you wish, Guinevere," smirked Henry, "We MUST save poor, poor Ferret!"

Henry turned and left the dorm room of Guinevere Uppington-Smythe. He made it almost halfway up the rickety back staircase before he burst into a raucous laughter.

Charlie The Yeti was in rare form. He wasn't used to "holding court", as it were, with everyone in attendance hanging on his every misbegotten word and, insomuch as he wished to butter up his new patrons in hopes of getting a feather pillow for his bed of hay and, perhaps, an additional snack during the afternoon. He laid it on thicker as he went.

"Whither comest me hither from thither," he pontificated in a faux operatic baritone, capering across the front of the Council Ring, occasionally lunging and snarling at a small cadre of First Years in the front row, eliciting audible gasps from the neophytes, then glancing back at the tribunal for signs of approval and, receiving indulgent smiles, blathering on, "These four Christmas hooligans have hounded me throughout the fabled realms of The Fade for no other reason than I be a friend to all druids and wish not to renounce my allegiance to your most magnanimous sect! They are a vexation! A pox upon them, says I! I'll not sully my paws on the likes of such as they!"

"Oh, poor Charlie," sobbed the now awake Carol, "I hope those mean people get what's coming to them!"

"He's talking about US, dummy!" spat Noel.

"Noel!" scolded Holly, "Don't call your sister names!"

Eve silently rolled her eyes. She was in no mood for silly fairy chitchat. Charlie continued his testimony.

"What choice, then, had I but to trespass on your resplendent campus, seeking succor and sanctuary? I ask you, most august assemblage, is that any way for a proud yeti to be treated? I say thee NAY!"

Much of Charlie's testimony was cribbed from a dog-eared copy of Shakespearian sonnets he stole from an American North Pole weather installation and pretty much all of it was a bald-faced lie. Despite that, when he finished and smugly took his seat, a buzz of approbation flooded the arena and reverberated off the rough-hewn stone columns. Charlie had the student body of Stonehenge Academy eating out of his hairy palm.

"Thank you, Charlie," said Custodian Homberg, indulgently, "We all have felt the sting of Christmas mayhem and weep for your tribulations! We welcome you to the safety of our bosoms."

"For my next witness," continued Homberg, "I call forth Headmaster Fraxineus!"

As Fraxineus rose and smoothed the front of his robe and straightened his stole, the tension in the gallery was palpable.

"Students, fellow faculty," Fraxineus stated flatly to the rapt audience, "In the wake of friend Charlie's most grandiloquent discourse, I fear my own testimony may be a bit tepid. However, as a key witness, I saw with my own eyes the four accused prisoners trespassing on Academy grounds, the old haunted grist mill by name, standing over a bound Charlie and wearing loud Christmas-themed regalia, flouting the sacrosanct Stonehenge Academy rules. Their guilt is incontrovertible!"

"Further," he continued, "Their only justification for their unlawful presence on druidic turf was the search for a mythic strand of garland purportedly in the possession of our boon yeti companion, which, I might add, remains an artifact no one has seen thus far. So ends my testimony."

"You have all heard the testimony regarding the charges against this Christmas Eve person and her obviously demonic companions," concluded Homberg, pointing towards Eve and the caged fairies, "The prosecution rests."

"Now, we will hear from you," barked 'He Whose Name Cannot Be Spoken', Llewellyn Magellan Quirinius McMillan (a.k.a. Lou), signaling the bailiff to remove Eve's gag and bring her forward to stand before the tribunal.

"Students and faculty of Stonehenge Academy," began Christmas Eve.

"Lies! Vicious falsehoods!" roared Charlie, leaping to his feet, "Burn the witch! Burn them all!"

"That's not how we do things around here, friend Charlie," admonished Fraxineus.

"And yet the notion has some merit," interjected Excentrus Dowergoth calmly.

"I'd say things couldn't possibly get any worse," thought Eve to herself, "But I've been around long enough to know better."

END CHAPTER FIFTEEN

Chapter Sixteen

Henry Cobbler raced down the winding corridors leading to a little used entrance located behind the dais of Salisbury Amphitheater, carefully avoiding any potential run-ins with faculty, staff or students who decided to skip the proceedings and wander the halls of Stonehenge Academy, opting for a "free period" instead. As he stealthily crept towards the back door to the arena, he felt inside his school blazer for the Golden Garland, to make sure it was still there and to reassure himself that he was doing the right thing facing down the entire faculty and student body of Stonehenge Academy in an attempt to simply put things right.

"Stiff upper lip, Henry," the boy encouraged himself, "Right is right, after all, and the Christmas people certainly didn't ask for any of this! Besides, what's the worst they could do to you?"

Henry's rhetorical question sent his mind whirling into all sorts of dire scenarios, most of which ended with some variation of him being crushed beneath a gigantic granite slab with Ferret and Guinevere laughing and dancing atop the slab and waving the garland in the breeze while the rest of the school looked on.

Henry tried to push these thoughts from his brain as he reached the door, unlatched it, and opened it ever so slightly ajar, supposing the low creak it made as it opened sounded very much like a rusty guillotine being hoisted into position. As he peered into the vast amphitheater, he saw Christmas Eve addressing the assemblage.

Christmas Eve could be tactful when the situation required it, but she was no diplomat. She needed to tread carefully where this druidic conclave was concerned. She was not so much concerned for her own well-being but, rather that of her caged Sugar Plum companions and, too, the future of Santa's entire worldwide operations. She simply must convince the druids of the rightness of her cause and their overall innocence and that required the correct, specific testimony.

"Ladies and gentlemen, faculty and esteemed tribunal," she began, "The charges and evidence presented here today, while technically true… for the most part…"

Eve shot Charlie a withering glance which silenced him momentarily from interrupting her testimony a second time. Eve continued.

"Yet there is much circumstantial information and outright MIS-information that needs to be cleared up, and CAN be with a simple explanation."

"Yeah! First off, Charlie is a great big FIBBER!" howled Carol from her cage.

"He wears those lederhosen because his pants caught on fire!" yelled Noel.

"What does that mean… oh, wait! I get it! Good one, Noel!" chimed in Holly.

"Girls, please!" interjected Eve, noticing the sour looks on the faces of the tribunal. They were not amused by silly fairy antics.

"Excuse my friends, good sirs, they mean no disrespect" soothed

Eve, "They're nervous and, perhaps, a bit rambunctious, but they're not wrong. Charlie IS a reprehensible misanthrope!"

"HEY!" snarled Charlie, "I'm sitting right here!"

"That's downright hurtful," he simpered, trying his best to make puppy dog eyes and a quivering lower lip for the benefit of the assemblage.

"Please dispense with the insensitive name calling, you vile holiday co-opting witch!" reproached Headmaster Fraxineus, apparently oblivious to the irony of his own statement.

"Sorry, your lordship," acquiesced Eve, "As I was saying, I believe this whole matter can be cleared up with a simple, straightforward explanation."

The tribunal halfheartedly signaled Eve to continue with her testimony, obviously bored with the entire proceedings by this point. They wanted it to be over and a judgement rendered as soon as humanly possible. The spectators in the gallery weren't much better. Most had already made up their minds and were sure nothing this Christmas woman could say would change their opinions. Some were already nodding off. Others were talking amongst themselves about sports or upcoming tests. A few of the First Years were preoccupied with a big, green insect that was skittering across the front of the raised platform where the dais was situated, trying to change its path with a piece of straw. One older faculty member was snoring loudly, delighting the students around him no end. Eve stoically soldiered on in spite of the distractions. Only Henry Cobbler, still hunkered down in the doorway seemed at all interested in her story.

Eve tried to keep her version of events brief and on point. Still, the scope and expanse of her tale was starting to capture the attention of some of the audience. Most of them had never been outside the confines of Stonehenge Academy and her retelling of encounters with elder gods and musketeers and knights and detectives in various other regions within The Fade were enthralling and fascinating. By the time her dissertation was over, she had won over much of the audience. But, was it enough? The tribunal looked as stern as ever. It was judgement time!

Headmaster Fraxineus, Custodian Homberg and Excentrus Dowergoth rose as one. Dowergoth elbowed 'He Whose Name Cannot Be Spoken', Llewellyn Magellan Quirinius McMillan (a.k.a. Lou), who had been daydreaming, and he quickly followed suit. The most august tribunal of Stonehenge Academy was about to pass judgement.

"We have heard testimony on both sides of the matter at hand," began Fraxineus piously, "And we find both tales equally compelling."

"Some more so than others," interjected Custodian Homberg sourly, directing a withering gaze in Christmas Eve's direction.

"Homberg, please!" scolded Excentrus Dowergoth, "Allow the Headmaster to proceed!"

"What he said," added 'He Whose Name Cannot Be Spoken', Llewellyn Magellan Quirinius McMillan (a.k.a. Lou), having nothing cogent to add but not wishing to be left out of the conversation.

"Thank you, gentlemen," replied Fraxineus peevishly.

"In any event," he continued, "The crux of this contretemps seems to center around the mythical Golden Garland Of Zeus, which the accused Christmas troublemakers claim our new comrade, Charlie, has stolen from public enemy number one, him known as Santa Claus. However, Charlie vehemently denies the charges and the accused have as yet failed to present said garland as evidence in their defense."

"A base canard of the highest order!" spat Custodian Homberg, "A mere ruse perpetrated to deflect attention away from their own obvious guilt!"

"I fear I must concur," interposed Excentrus Dowergoth, "Without the swag in question, the entirety of the given testimony is inadmissible hearsay!"

"Hearsay, heresy, it's all the same in my book," chuckled 'He Whose Name Cannot Be Spoken', Llewellyn Magellan Quirinius McMillan (a.k.a. Lou).

Charlie the Yeti wasn't quite sure what many of those big words meant, but he liked their accusatory tone. Things seemed to be going his way and he did his best to stifle a smug, self-satisfied smile, trying to feign as much innocence as he could muster.

"We are in agreement, then, it seems," alleged Headmaster Fraxineus, uncaringly, "So, I ask you again, for the final time, Christmas Eve, do you have possession of or know the whereabouts of this Golden Garland Of Zeus?"

"I'm sorry, sir, I do not," replied Eve dejectedly.

"In that case," pronounced Fraxineus, the entire arena hanging on his every word, "You leave us no choice but to declare thusly… for the crimes of trespassing, licentiousness and wanton promotion of the hated Christmas holiday, we, the tribunal of Stonehenge Academy and the druidic nation at large, find you and your fairy friends guilt -- *"

"Wait!" shouted Henry Cobbler, rising from his hiding place and producing the Golden Garland from beneath his blazer, "I have Exhibit A right here, your honors!"

END CHAPTER SIXTEEN

Chapter Seventeen

The full ramifications of Henry Cobbler's actions were beginning to dawn on the young student. This was his school and these were his people. He should have been in agreement with the majority. They had their reasons for detesting Christmas, regardless of how archaic those reasons may be. And, too, Henry really only had two friends at the academy, Ferret Reynolds and Guinevere Uppington-Smythe. Most of the rest of the student body and quite a few of the faculty and staff regarded him with dismissive contempt for his having been raised by Celtlings, an upbringing he bore through no fault of his own.

In any event, it would have been quite easy for Henry to have remained quiet until after the judgement was passed and the sentence was carried out. Then, he could have snuck out to the woods and burned the swag to ashes or buried it at the very least, with no one the wiser. So easy.

But, there stood Henry, in front of the assembled multitude of Stonehenge Academy, waving the accursed swag in the air and shouting "Exhibit A! Exhibit A!" like some sort of crazed lunatic.

"What is the meaning of this interruption?" bellowed Headmaster Fraxineus, "I seem to recall having you confined to quarters, Mr. Cobbler!"

"And what is that ratty boa you're waving about, Henry?" roared Custodian Homberg.

Explain yourself, Cobbler!" snarled Excentrus Dowergoth.

"And it better be good!" japed 'He Whose Name Cannot Be Spoken', Llewellyn Magellan Quirinius McMillan (a.k.a. Lou).

Seeing the garland on full display and his subsequent chances for a cushy life in the Stonehenge Menagerie slipping away, Charlie the Yeti rose slowly to a crouching position, eyes darting furtively around the room for the nearest exit.

"Sit down, Charlie!" admonished Eve, pushing firmly down on Charlie's shoulder until his rear end hit the stone floor with a dull thud.

"This is the golden garland everyone is going on about, Head-master," offered Henry, "I found it, um, lodged under the paddle-wheel at the old haunted gristmill."

That, of course, was not the truth of it but, although he had lost all respect and feelings of love for her, Henry, nonetheless, did not wish to get Guinevere in any more trouble than she was already in for following him and Ferret on their yeti hunt. She was still one of his only friends, after all.

"Way to go, Henry!" cheered Holly from her cage.

"Hmmph! 'Bout time you showed up, kid," groused Noel.

"Did you bring any fudge with you, Henry?" asked Carol, "I'm hungry and I LOVE fudge!"

"Hush, girls," chided Eve, "It's nice to see you again, Henry Cob-bler. May I have the Golden Garland, please?"

Henry handed the Golden Garland Of Zeus to Christmas Eve who turned immediately to the tribunal and held the aureate swag towards them.

"This is the Golden Garland Of Zeus, your honors! The very relic we have been searching for across the depth and breadth of The Fade. The one that was stolen from Santa Claus by Charlie the Yeti," announced Eve.

"Oh, you'd like them to believe THAT," snarled Charlie, rising to his feet now that Eve was no longer next to him to keep him seated and obedient, "It's a pretty piece of fluff, I'll grant you, but it is no more than a minor DECORATION!"

As a low murmur began to work its way through the crowd, Charlie felt a wave of smug confidence welling up inside. He was faking, sure, but the student body seemed to be eating it up with a knife and fork. Chicanery was second nature to the wily yeti and he was delighting in this turn of events. He decided to press his advantage.

"I mean, come on," Charlie continued audaciously, "Golden garland of Zeus? REALLY? The ancient Greeks didn't even celebrate Christmas, so how would someone like Zeus be aware of things like garland and tinsel? Why, you might as well say that the "thing" she's holding is… is… your Aunt Sophie's feathered boa!"

Charlie quickly sat down, hoping that someone in that assemblage actually had an Aunt Sophie and that she was a bit flamboyant. Nonetheless, the damage was done. The seeds of "reasonable doubt" were sown. The tribunal began to huddle together and started muttering amongst themselves, those who had beards stroking them thoughtfully. The girls slumped down in their cages in gloomy defeat. If Eve, holding the evidence in her hand, couldn't convince them of the truth of her story, how would they ever get out of there and back to Christmas Valley?

"Order! Order!" roared Headmaster Fraxineus, sensing the proceeding getting somewhat out of order and wishing to restore calm, "Seniors contain the First Years and you Middle Years should know better!"

Headmaster Fraxineus turned towards the others on the tribunal and offered his take on Charlie's testimony and the new evidence that Henry Cobbler put before the court.

"Charlie is our friend, for one," he opined, "And we all know the depths to which those Christmas people will stoop to get their own way. Centuries of lies, theft and abuse have taught us that."

"Still, we don't know friend Charlie long enough to get a true sense of his character," added Excentrus Dowergoth, "And what advantage would this Christmas Eve person hope to gain by fostering such a canard?"

"I say we execute the lot of them, Charlie included," chirped 'He Whose Name Cannot Be Spoken', Llewellyn Magellan Quirinius McMillan (a.k.a. Lou), "The granite slab is big enough to accommodate them all. Those fairies don't take up all that much room."

"Food for thought," said Custodian Homberg, his voice trailing off as he and the others gave 'He Whose Name Cannot Be Spoken', Llewellyn Magellan Quirinius McMillan (a.k.a. Lou) a quizzical side glance.

"In any event," continued Excentrus Dowergoth, "We need to reach a unanimous verdict and soon. The student body is getting restless and I fear won't sit for much more of our dithering."

With that admonition ringing in his ears, Headmaster Fraxineus rose to his feet, straightened his robe, cleared his throat and began the short walk to the front of the dais. He was just about to speak when a sudden storm broke out over the amphitheater and lightning began flashing all around. The student body started scrambling for what meager cover they could find, hunkering down next to their stone seats.

Suddenly, to the back of the theater, a blinding flash of lightning heralded the appearance of two regal looking forms.

"Hera! Zeus!," called Eve above the howling wind.

"Uh, oh," swallowed Charlie.

"Hello, Eve," intoned Hera calmly.

"Who doubts the veracity of my golden swag?" thundered Zeus.

Charlie was uncertain if it was the static from the lightning or un-bridled fear that made the hair on his entire body stand on end. Either way, he was in trouble.

END CHAPTER SEVENTEEN

Chapter Eighteen

Zeus and Hera approached the dais imperially, lightning still crackling about them. The tribunal sat silently. The rest of the assemblage cowered in awestruck wonder at the sudden appearance of the Greek deities. Only Christmas Eve had the courage to step forward and greet the rulers of the ancient Greek pantheon.

"I'm certainly glad to see you both," effused Eve, "But, I thought you had a strict policy about interfering in another realms affairs?"

"Ah, my dear Christmas Eve," bellowed Zeus, "That is generally our procedure but we are here, not as invaders, but as witnesses and, as such, claim the rights of diplomatic immunity!"

"Everything will be fine, dear," said Hera calmly, shooting Eve a knowing wink.

"Order! Order!" shouted Headmaster Fraxineus over the cacophonous clangor of fearfully whimpering students and the loud thunder booms and crackling lightning, "State your business, Mighty Zeus, and then be gone! Your 'diplomatic immunity', like my patience has its limits!"

"By your own admission, your godlike powers hold no sway here in our domain," added Excentrus Dowergoth.

Lightning flashed in Zeus's eyes at this perceived affront and a full blown storm began welling up in him until Hera's firm hand on his shoulder soothed his mercurial temperament.

"Use your words, dear," she cooed.

"My 'business', as you so crudely put it, is to right a wrong and redress the impugning of my veracity!" snarled Zeus.

The imperious Greek ruler from Olympus went on to explain that, in spite of Charlie's assertion to the contrary, that the swag Eve held was, indeed, the actual Golden Garland Of Zeus and it was as genuine as the legends had proclaimed. His testimony being received by the assemblage with Oohs and Ahhs of approbation, Zeus turned to leave. As he crossed the dais, he began shaking his hand and rubbing his wrist.

"I seem to have developed a cramp," cried Zeus.

At that proclamation, a small lightning bolt shot out from the hand in question and sliced its way across the dais and shattered the three locks on the Sugar Plum Fairies' respective cages.

"Oh, Fiddlesticks," minced Zeus, "I hate when that happens!"

"Oh, you big growly bear! In spite of your slothful, lecherous ways, it's moments like this that remind me of why I love you!" chuckled Hera as she threw her arms about her king and kissed him playfully on his cheek.

"Please, dearest! Not in front of the Druids!" teased Zeus.

With that, the pair vanished as abruptly as they had appeared with nothing to mark their departure save a distant rumbling of thunder and the faint smell of ozone in the air. Meanwhile, Holly, Noel and Carol joined Eve and Henry Cobbler on stage, where the quintet stared down the tribunal, waiting for them to continue with their verdict.

"You were saying?" chirped Eve.

Henry Cobbler stood before the gnarled wooden door that was Stonehenge's gateway into and out of The Fade. What a momentous day this had been! Following the appearance of Zeus and Hera, the tribunal received a parade of "visitors", all claiming diplomatic immunity and all wishing to testify on Christmas Eve's behalf and, in many cases, against Charlie The Yeti. Musketeers, wizards, detectives, mad scientists and even Rumpelstiltskin (a.k.a. Sprinkles) gave witness to Eve's quest and Charlie's skullduggery.

In light of such testimony, the tribunal had little choice but to free the Christmas heroine and her fairy charges, grant her access to their doorway back to the real world and allow her to retain possession of the Golden Garland, with the provision that they go as quickly as possible and NEVER return to Stonehenge Academy under any circumstances.

For her part, Eve promised to update Santa's map so that his route through The Fade would circumvent the Druidic section regardless of the free passage the garland afforded him. Christmas, she told them, is about inclusion, not exclusion and, until they could staunch their enmity towards Christmas, there was no good reason to rub their noses in it once a year.

"I wouldn't mind it, though, if a candy cane or two found its way here once in a while," added 'He Whose Name Cannot Be Spoken', Llewellyn Magellan Quirinius McMillan (a.k.a. Lou).

But, what to do about Charlie The Yeti, they all opined. Christmas Eve, in spite of everything, advocated forgiveness. That was the Christmas way, after all. The Sugar Plum Fairies reluctantly agreed, with only Noel lobbying for a good spanking for the hairy lout.

Their dilemma was solved with the last minute arrival of Uncle Grimfang who insisted that Charlie be remanded into his custody. He contended that it was Charlie's actions that caused his village to be destroyed by the Huns and Charlie should be the one to rebuild it. The tribunal and Christmas Eve all agreed to this work release program.

"An' don't you worry none, Christmas Gal," chuckled Uncle Grimfang, "When he's done with that little chore, there's plenty more to keep him busy and out of mischief… boulders to be moved, aqueducts to be constructed, fields to be plowed… oh, he's gonna be busy for a long time!"

So, with all that settled, there was only one more thing to deal with… Henry Cobbler.

"Why don't you come with us," offered Eve, "You'd be more that welcome in Santa's Village."

"Yes, Henry! Please come!" pleaded Holly, "You really helped us out of a jam!"

"Yeah!" added Noel, "You're way cooler than these other Druid stiffs!"

"We can make fudge together, Henry," chirped Carol, "I LOVE fudge!"

"Thank you all for your kind offer," replied Henry, "But the students and faculty of Stonehenge have just gotten their first taste of Christmas wonder and good cheer and if I left, who would there be to foster that belief? No, I think I have a job ahead of me. I'll start them off slowly… maybe a secular Christmas song… Jingle Bells, perhaps?"

"Bravo, Henry Cobbler! You'll make a splendid Christmas ambassador for The Fade!" smiled Eve, hugging the boy and kissing him on the forehead right next to his Ferret-induced cricket bat scar.

And, with that, Christmas Eve, accompanied by Holly Noel and Carol, departed through the door, fading into mist ever so slowly as they returned to the real world.

"Goodbye, my new friends," said Henry with a small tear glistening in the corner of his eye, "I hope we may meet again one day for tea and scones… and fudge."

END CHAPTER EIGHTEEN

Chapter Nineteen

It was the morning of Christmas Eve day and Santa was worriedly tapping his gloved hand on the front of his sleigh. In hopes to facilitate things and, too, because Mrs. Claus banished him from the workshop for the remainder of the day to keep his nervous fretting from infecting the jolly nature of the last minute preparations, Santa had harnessed up Blitzen and driven the sleigh to the dilapidated stile out by the rill and copse of evergreens.

"They also serve who only sit and wait," Santa halfheartedly chortled to Blitzen, who reassuringly nickered back.

"I worry that maybe this mission was just too much for even an accomplished Christmas super heroine like Christmas Eve," sighed Santa, "And letting her take those sweet little fairies with her to that dangerous place without the benefit of the Golden Garland… what was I thinking?"

"Well, Blitzen, old man, it's getting to be about noon. I suppose we should go back and break the sad news to everyone that for the first time in my many years of doing this job we'll just have to cancel our trip," lamented Santa, "The whole castle will be heartbroken but we simply can't risk it without our protective swag."

As Santa slumped into his seat and grabbed up the reins, he heard a faint rustling coming from the direction of the old turnstile.

It started as barely a whisper but slowly got louder. It was the sound of a cloak flapping in the wind. The jolly one turned to see Christmas Eve and the girls slowly begin to come into focus… and Eve was holding the Golden Garland Of Zeus in her hands!

"HO HO HO!" laughed Santam "Leave it to you, Christmas Eve, to wait until the last minute to save the day!"

"Actually, there are several hours left," replied Holly officiously.

"We can go back and wait until sundown if you'd like, Santa," giggled Noel impishly.

"Now, girls, be nice!" reprimanded Eve, "Here's your Golden Garland, Santa, no worse for wear."

"Splendid!" chortled Santa jollily, "Tell, me, did you have much trouble?"

"Oh, do we have a story to tell you, Santa!" warbled Holly gleefully.

"Really? Well, maybe you'd better tell me back at the castle over lunch," said Santa Claus.

"But… but…" stammered Carol.

"Yes, Carol, there will be fudge!" sighed Santa wistfully.

"Oh. Goody! Let's go," yelled Carol as off she flew.

Later that day, after a hearty lunch that included seven different kinds of fudge, Christmas Eve told everyone at Santa's castle all about their adventures in The Fade, with the girls acting out the more thrilling parts. Soon, though, it was time for Santa to leave on his ride. He kissed his wife goodbye, gave Eve a big hug and a small present and he gave a Christmas stocking to each Sugar Plum Fairy (Carol's contained fudge). Then, with a flick of the reins and a hearty "Ho Ho Ho" he was off to spread Christmas joy to the whole world.

"I LOVE this job," said Christmas Eve with a huge grin.

"And I love this fudge," mumbled Carol through a mouthful of the sweet treat.

"Let's go, girls," remarked Eve as she shushed the three fairies out of Santa's castle towards their chalet headquarters, "Santa won't come if you're not in bed!"

"Oh, like THAT's gonna happen," snorted Noel, "He owes us BIG!"

"Noel!" scolded Holly.

"Well, he does," continued Noel.

"Sigh, let's go, girls," huffed an exhausted and exasperated Christmas Eve.

Charlie The Yeti was down on his aching knees, trying to attach two boards to one another with a bent nail and a rock. He had been working on rebuilding the Tibetan Yetis' village all day without rest and dusk was setting in. Through his fatigue and much swearing, Charlie heard the faint sound of jingle bells approaching. He dropped his rock, stood up stiffly and looked up just in time to see Santa Claus and his team coming in for a landing right in his recently cleared out front yard.

"Hello, Charlie," warbled Santa cheerfully.

"What?" groused Charlie, "Come to gloat, have you?"

"Far from it," replied Santa, "I've come to present you with this," he said, pulling a brightly wrapped gift from the back of his sleigh.

"What's this for?" grumbled Charlie, "I did you dirt. Why would you give me a present? Is there a poisonous snake in here?"

"I didn't think you'd understand. Maybe you never will, but everyone deserves a gift on Christmas, even a miserable wretch like you. You're taking your punishment like a man, so to speak, and I'm here to offer forgiveness," explained Santa, "Now, if you'll excuse me, I have a schedule to keep!"

As Santa flew off on his rounds, Charlie ripped open the gift box to find a brand new tool belt inside with a shiny new hammer and saw and wrench and screwdriver and nails and everything. As he stood there, dumbfounded, staring at his gift, his Uncle Grimfang came bursting out of the hovel.

"What's all the ruckus out here, nephew?" snarled Uncle Grimfang, "Who were you talking to?"

"No one," replied Charlie dreamily, "No one at all."

"What's wrong with you, boy?" queried Uncle Grimfang?

"Me? Plenty," snapped Charlie sardonically, "But, just for tonight, everything is all right!"

As Grimfang stormed crankily back into their home, Charlie observed softly, "Merry Christmas, Uncle."

THE END

About The Author

GEORGE J. BRODERICK, JR. began cartooning at age five when he peddled drawings of Mighty Mouse, Woody Woodpecker and Popeye from the back of his little red wagon to the unsuspecting neighborhood moms for a nickel a sketch (which George still considers one of the highlights of his freelance career).

George has worked as a professional in comics since 1982. Since then, he has written stories for DC Comics, Marvel Comics and handled both scripting and editing on the LOST IN SPACE and QUANTUM LEAP comic books for Innovation Publishing and editing on LOST IN SPACE: Voyage to the Bottom of the Soul for Bubblehead Publishing.

George's art credits include work on BOZO THE CLOWN and SANTA CLAUS ADVENTURES for Innovation, SPEED RACER for Now Comics and THE MUNSTERS for TV Comics, the RADIOACTIVE MAN and LURE LASS/WEASEL WOMAN features in SIMPSON'S SUPER SPECTACULAR for Bongo Comics, MUMMIES, GHOSTS, KOLCHAK, THE NIGHT STALKER and SUCKULINA, VAMPIRE TEMP for Moonstone Books, LIFE MAXX for A Way With Words Foundation, POPEYE THE SAILOR for Premium Pop Comics/CLI 2.0. His most current work includes SUPER DUPER TALES, SUPER DUPER FUNNIES, SUPER DUPER COMICS & STORIES, SUPER DUPER ADVENTURES, SCINTILLATING TALES, THE BIG BOOK OF CHRISTMAS EVE, THE GREAT BIG BOOK OF CHRISTMAS LEGENDS, HOLLY JOLLY CHRISTMAS COMICS, THE QUACK QUACK DIARIES, DRAGONFACE VISITS THE DENTIST, MR. CRANKY PANTS PLANTS A GARDEN and MISTER BUNDLES VS. THE MARTIANS for CLI 2.0.

George currently creates and posts web comics appearing five days a week, HOLY COW COMICS, a cornucopia of random strips updated Monday through Friday at: http://www.townburgcity.com.

George's biggest ambition in life is to become one of the most beloved characters in American Folklore!